What the critics saying:

...hot, graphically explicit...Jan Springer really knows how to heat up a love scene to the sizzling point! ~ *Donna, eCataRomance Reviews*

...sassy humor and passionate sex...simply outstanding...4 ½ hearts! - *Renee Burnette , The Romance Studio*

...a hot, steamy story that lives up to its E-rotic rating... ~ *Patti Fischer, Romance Reviews Today*

A Hero Betrayed will make you sweat with the heat of passion and cheer with joy... ~ *Jenni, A Romance Review*

...one HOT story...arousing and erotic...a must read... ~ *Ruby, Fallen Angel Reviews*

...4 stars!...hot and heavy...definitely looking for more from this author ~ *Julie Bryan, Just Erotic Romance Reviews*

ELLORA'S CAVE
ROMANTICA PUBLISHING

A HERO BETRAYED
An Ellora's Cave Publication, September 2004

Ellora's Cave Publishing, Inc.
PO Box 787
Hudson, OH 44236-0787

ISBN #1-4199-5042-8

ISBN MS Reader (LIT) ISBN # 1-84360-858-8
Other available formats (no ISBNs are assigned):
Adobe (PDF), Rocketbook (RB), Mobipocket (PRC) & HTML

Edited by *Raelene Gorlinsky*
Cover art by *Darrell King*

HEROES AT HEART:
A HERO BETRAYED

Jan Springer

Dedication:

For Raelene Gorlinski, a great editor.

And for my dar buddy, Tracey West, who suggested a sensual watermelon scene for this book to celebrate the joys of watermelon sex. Enjoy!

Chapter One

On the planet of Paradise…

Flames of pain licked United States Astronaut Buck Hero's tender flesh as the harsh whip snapped across his bare buttocks with such force, he couldn't stop himself from crying out.

He preferred blondes but this was ridiculous.

Five blonde females stood nude in a semi-circle in front of him. Of varying heights, all looked quite healthy with tanned skin and generous curves. Lust brewed in their excited gazes as they watched him getting whipped.

He wished he could share in their excitement. Unfortunately, having them ogling his tortured naked body was kind of embarrassing.

Being a creature of comfort, he preferred a nice fluffy bed with romantic candlelight illuminating the luscious body of one curvy woman who was eager to tend to his sexual needs.

Instead, thick ropes descended from a sturdy branch overhead and tangled around his wrists, stretching his arms way too tight as his body dangled by his screaming shoulders. Not to mention his legs were spread-eagled, ankles tied tightly with ropes that led to stakes pounded into the ground.

Who the heck would have guessed he'd get caught by a group of sex-crazed females with a whipping fetish while he was undertaking a top-secret scientific NASA exploration mission on a planet millions of miles from Earth. If there ever was a time he needed help from his two missing brothers, this would be it.

At the rate of pain searing throughout his body parts, he was just about ready to submit to whatever they wanted. And by the seductive way those young women licked their full lips, stroked their shaven cunts and cupped their generous breasts, he could easily figure out what it was they were after.

He held his breath as the five young women moved in closer.

From behind him the air whistled as the sixth female, also a blonde, lowered the whip yet again.

Buck tried to tense against the incoming attack. This time the strike seared against his upper right shoulder. Before he could cry out from the wicked pain, a hot mouth clamped over the head of his semi-erect shaft and he cursed the pleasant feelings the young woman's hot eager mouth slowly built in his cock and balls.

Fighting his restraints proved futile. The woman who'd devoured his cock merely chuckled around his flesh. Her suckling sounds soon intermingled with another whisper of the whip, making him groan with frustration as pain once again smacked his buttocks.

Up until now he'd kept his mouth shut. Had obediently followed NASA's protocol at keeping a low profile and obeying his brother Ben's last communication when he'd warned Buck that the men on this planet weren't educated enough to speak more than a few sentences at best.

Speak or not, when a woman started sucking him off without his permission, it was time to break the silence.

"Get off me!"

His harsh shout did the trick. The woman released his rod with a pop and fell back on her butt with a dull thud. The whipping stopped immediately. All the women stared at him, wide-eyed with shock.

"Now that I've got your attention, please release me and I'll forget this unfortunate incident ever happened."

No one moved to do his bidding. They simply stared at him as if he were some sort of alien from another planet. Which he was, but that didn't give them the excuse for bad manners.

Finally the tallest of the blondes broke the quiet of the late evening.

"Looks like we've caught ourselves a talking male."

"That's right honey. Now I'm ordering you to cut me down this minute or there will be hell to pay."

"There's a large bounty on the head of a talking male," another whispered, ignoring his command.

"Screw your bounty. I demand you to let me go."

"He must be one of those escaped educated sex slaves from last year's Slave Uprising."

Oh great! They thought he was a sex slave.

"Sex slaves are experts at pleasuring women," the cutest of the six said.

The women's blue gazes all brightened as they watched him curiously.

Uneasiness zipped up Buck's spine.

"Sorry ladies, but this guy ain't a sex slave. He's a free man, or at least I will be in a minute when you let me go."

"Quiet, slave, or it'll be the whip again!" the tall blonde snapped angrily.

Ookay, he could shut up. For a minute.

"We are not giving up this well-endowed male or the fun we've planned for ourselves just for a bounty!" The tall blonde addressed the others. Buck's hopes were dashed as all eagerly nodded in agreement.

The tall blonde spoke again, her harsh blue gaze clashed defiantly with Buck's. "And I, for one, do not want a male speaking while I fuck him. Perchance I should cut out his tongue?"

He didn't miss her hand slithering to the dagger strapped to her leg. Have mercy! These women were crazy!

"I have a better idea," another blonde chimed in. "We'll give him the passion poison now."

"The elders have warned 'tis dangerous to administer it without their guidance," one of them said quickly.

"But it will make him more obedient and quiet until they arrive," the tall blonde replied thoughtfully.

Oh man, he was screwed. Hopefully not literally.

"I'm up for a little danger." The woman who'd attacked his dick with an eager mouth grinned widely.

"I'm not interested!" Buck gasped as a whisper of panic threatened his sanity. "Cut me down. I've about had enough of this crap!"

The women's harsh intakes of breath made Buck tense. Obviously they didn't like being ordered around. The feminist movement was very much alive and well on this planet.

"The passion poison it is." The tall blonde smiled with smug satisfaction. From behind him he sensed movement. Before he could react, a sharp sting from a needle pierced the flesh of his right ass cheek.

He tried to swing himself away, but couldn't move more than a few inches.

He swore violently as the cool liquid flooded deep into his veins and spread an odd sensual heat throughout his tortured body.

The heat soothed the fiery whip welts, and languid weariness drifted through his limbs. He fought hard to keep his suddenly heavy eyelids from closing but knew he was quickly losing the battle.

"He's getting sleepy," the blonde who'd been sucking his cock giggled.

"It's too bad we'll have to kill him when we're through with him," someone else said. "His size would bring a fortune in the Brothel Town."

They were going to kill him? Oh boy, he'd really stepped into big-time trouble.

The whirring sound of the whip sliced through the air yet again and he gritted his teeth as savage pain snapped against his bare buttocks. This time however, the pain was brief, turning quickly into a savage erotic sensation that made Buck groan with want for more.

"It's working," a female uttered from somewhere nearby.

He shook his head to clear his fogging thoughts, but all that accomplished was giving one of the women free rein on his earlobe. She pressed a lusciously soft breast against his elbow as she nibbled on his flesh. Her warm silky hands slid wantonly over his sweaty chest until a hot ache throbbed throughout his body.

He found himself moaning at the wonderful sensations and to his horror he found himself craving more pleasure. His cock and balls grew painfully hard. He heard the women's sharp gasps and excited giggles.

"I've never seen a male so big!" one of them screamed.

"Take him down," another instructed in a rather hoarse voice. "Let's get him into the hide house. We'll get the Sacred Drink from him and then we'll let him rest. When he is fully adjusted to the passion poison, we're going to become women!"

Wild cheers pierced the warm evening air.

As they freed his limp legs, United States astronaut Buck Hero succumbed to the black tidal wave of sleep that swallowed him whole.

* * * * *

Sexual tension hung heavy in the air as Buck gazed through the opening of the hide house.

Outside, his six captors danced frantically around a sparking bonfire not more than twenty feet away. Each woman carried a knife, their hands reaching to the dark sky as they chanted. Their bare breasts bobbed fiercely in the firelight and strange looking bone necklaces and amulets bounced around their necks as they stamped their feet and swayed their curvy hips in sensual movements.

If they were trying to turn him on, they were doing a darn fine job of it. The cock ring they'd nestled snugly over his cock and balls while he'd slept was doing its job too. His package was so tight with arousal that pain lanced through his scrotum area. His shaft was a swollen purple, as hard as glass and near to bursting as it stuck straight into the air like an iron bar waiting for the women to take their turns with him.

He licked his dry lips as mixed emotions seesawed through him. One minute he couldn't wait for one of those women to mount him. The next minute he knew he had to get out of here.

And fast.

He pulled hard against his bonds. Nothing budged.

Damn!

Once again ropes held him captive. But this time they'd laid him on his back, spread-eagled him out on a dirt floor in the middle of what appeared to be a seven foot high, eight foot by eight foot animal-hide-covered structure framed by thick wood branches.

If this building was an indication, perhaps these ladies weren't as evolved as Earthlings. On the other hand, if this passion poison they'd injected him with was a warning, they might be more advanced than things appeared.

He swore he could feel the poison literally flowing through his veins. It gave him a lusty, sexually aroused kind of feeling that encouraged his body to tingle pleasantly all over. It showered him with a sexual awareness that made his cock feel like it would explode if one of those blonde bombshells didn't start fucking him soon.

Buck cursed beneath his breath and blinked with shock at the thought of wanting one of those young chicks riding him. There was no way he was going to let any of them near him. It simply wasn't proper for a United States astronaut to submit to these lusty cravings no matter what the reason. He would just have to figure a way out of these restraints.

Outside, the females suddenly shrieked in unison like a bunch of wild animals, making Buck stiffen against his bonds. He didn't have to be a genius to realize they were nearing the end of some sort of ritual dance.

He had no idea how long he'd been unconscious or how long they'd been dancing but by the way their bodies glistened with perspiration as they gyrated wildly around the bonfire, they'd been at it for quite some time.

Transfixed by the erotic sight, he watched as the knives they carried in their hands sliced downwards and the women began slashing their upper arms with slow careful strokes, mutilating their silky skin.

Blood dripped from their wounds and they wasted no time in catching the red liquid in small wooden bowls.

Buck cursed silently. Obviously they had some sort of voodoo ritual going on here along with death threats.

It made it even more imperative he find a way out of these bonds.

Suddenly a sexy fragrance drifted through the air. It accelerated his heart rate and sent a sweet need through his senses.

He moaned out loud at the torturous impact.

Was this reaction an effect of the passion poison? Or something else?

The scent grew thicker, more intense. It curled deep into his lungs.

Lust cascaded over him in dark, sensuous waves until he felt as if he might scream out loud from his arousal.

A wave of fear zipped along his nerve endings. What in the world was happening to him? He'd never felt so aroused, so eager to be mounted, so emotionally aware in his life.

Without warning, a warm silky hand clamped firmly over his mouth. He blinked in surprise as he discovered a woman staring down at him with piercing pale blue eyes.

Damn! Just his luck.

Another blonde.

The strange panicky feeling zipped away as he realized she wasn't a part of the group of women who'd captured him.

He would have remembered this jewel.

She wore the most erotic clothing he'd ever seen. Well, maybe clothing wasn't the right word. More like…sexy transparent lingerie. Gauzy little shorts and quite the most revealing bikini top draped a luscious looking body.

His pulse skittered as he noted a quiver of arrows peeking over a sensually curved shoulder and the bow in her hand.

Definitely a female version of Robin Hood. How nice.

The flickering firelight seeping through the open doorway touched the gentle contours of her silky skin. Her hair was shoulder-length. Bangs feathered the tips of perfectly arched dark eyebrows. Long black lashes framed her wide set eyes.

She possessed a pretty pert nose, and leaning as close to him as she was, he couldn't miss the rosy blush that swept across high cheekbones. But most of all, he loved the sensually curved cupid bow mouth. He wanted those sexy lips on him.

All over him.

A flush of savage heat streaked through his veins and his whole body felt as if it were on fire.

He wanted to claim this woman. Wanted to pull her against him. To impale her, to thrust his swollen cock deep into her warm cavern with firm, challenging strokes until the sexual tension in his body eased.

Oh boy. The passion poison was working big time.

Dizziness assailed his senses as he watched her place a finger to her lips, gesturing him to remain silent.

Buck nodded numbly.

Lifting her hand from his mouth, she said nothing as she continued to peer down at him. Her hot gaze trailed a scorching path over his face. He could almost feel the petal softness of her luscious lips caressing his mouth. Could sense the sexual tension blossoming between them. Noticed the curves of her breasts swell against the sheer garment that barely covered her lovely mounds. Even her nipples, nestled in the middle of dark areolas, seemed to stab at the delicate green material in an effort to escape and be taken by his mouth.

Sexual awareness surged proudly through him as her hungry gaze swept over the width of his shoulders, over his muscular chest and downward to rest on his throbbing cock.

The tips of her pretty lips tilted upward with an appreciative smile and then suddenly she whipped her attention to the open doorway.

He followed her gaze and noted with growing unease the six females had stopped dancing. Standing around the bonfire, they chattered anxiously as they poured their blood from the small bowls into a large one being passed around.

The newcomer's sweet smile promptly vanished and she moved quickly toward the open door.

Her movements were graceful yet determined as she scuttled on hands and knees across the ground. He fought to slow down his heavy breathing as he noted a firmly rounded ass barely concealed by the see-through shorts. The dark crack of her buttocks shimmered before his eyes and he groaned inwardly at the thought of plunging his aching shaft into her warm vagina from behind.

Oh yeah, he really did prefer blondes.

Chapter Two

Oh Goddess of Freedom!

One look into his lust-filled eyes and Virgin had almost changed her mind about rescuing the male. She'd never seen an infected male gaze at a woman quite that way. The look had sent an unexpected jolt of sexual awareness shooting through her veins. Liquid heat had quickly pooled between her legs leaving her with a craving for more of those delicious looks.

When she'd seen the virgins inject the passion poison into him, her hopes of using him to achieve her own goals had faltered. She'd been given a time limit to capture one of these talking males and now with this newest development she was in trouble.

Her first instinct had been to wait until the females were done with him and then snatch him away.

But the chances of one virgin killing him immediately after the traditional couplings made that idea too risky. She needed him too badly to simply leave him here to die at their hands.

Squatting beside the hide-house doorway, she studied the six females. A gentle wave of homesickness washed over her as she recognized their young faces. Over a year ago, when she'd been their elected High Queen, these Yellow Hair girls had been developing into women. Now here they were on their first Male Hunt capturing a male for the traditional Virgin Dance.

It hurt her to think she would ruin their fun by crashing their party and taking him away from them. They were chattering with such excitement at the prospect of mounting the male she really couldn't blame them for being so happy. He was an exceptional specimen with the longest, thickest cock she'd ever laid eyes on.

Her heart picked up speed as she peeked back at the captive. Firelight illuminated his naked spread-eagle figure. Perspiration dampened his flushed skin, enhancing his muscular physique. For the briefest moment she wondered how it would feel to be embraced in those strong muscular arms, to touch his flushed face and press her lips against his luscious mouth.

Or better yet to straddle his powerful thighs and guide his thick erection deep to her very core.

Virgin closed her eyes and gave herself a mental shake.

Insanity!

Most of her life she'd known she wanted to become a High Queen in order to change the laws to make life better for males and women. She'd trained herself into thinking like a High Queen, knowing that as one of them she would never be allowed to fuck a male.

She was supposed to be a superior woman, a leader who set an example for all women. A woman who could defy being contaminated by a mere male.

And now look at her.

She was a desperate escaped fugitive lusting after a passion-infected male. One she needed to kidnap.

The cheerful chattering of the girl-women ripped Virgin's attention back to them. She watched as they sipped the traditional Sacred Drink from the large wooden bowl.

"Do we have to tell the elders that he's a talking male when they come to witness the fucking ceremony?" one of the Yellow Hair youngsters asked as she licked the red sacred mixture from her lips and passed the large bowl to the next virgin.

"There are bounties on the talking males' heads," another young woman said. "Of course we need to tell them. The elders have said a few sex slaves escaped from last year's Slave Uprising. That male has to be one of them."

"Why tell anyone who he is?" The tallest of them spat. "He's a male and he has the best-looking cock I've ever seen. That's all that matters to us. Besides, what the elders won't know won't hurt them. We'll simply bind him with a ball and gag. And besides that, much fun awaits with this male and I'm not letting the passion poison go to waste. Nor am I breaking tradition by allowing the male to live afterwards."

Another Yellow Hair chimed in. "Did you see how big he is? I don't even know if I can stuff his entire cock inside me. But I sure am going to try."

All six of them giggled.

Another virgin asked, "How long before the male will be sexually obedient enough to fuck?"

"As soon as the elders show up—which will be soon. Hurry and finish the traditional drink and then we can pick sticks. The one who draws the shortest gets to go in there first."

Virgin's gaze flew to the eastern horizon. To the thin gray streaks of dawn. Morning was approaching fast and they needed to be long gone before daylight hit and the elders arrived.

She scampered back to the male.

Her breath backed up in her throat as the sensual curve of his lips lifted into a sweet smile the instant he saw her.

Oh sweet mercy!

His smile sure made her heart do some mighty strange flips.

"I need you to be very quiet or they'll hear. Do you understand?" she asked.

He nodded.

From the scabbard strapped to her right leg, Virgin slid out her knife and quickly cut the ties that bound his legs and arms.

His skin felt sizzling hot to the touch as she slid her hands beneath his arms and helped him into a seated position.

"Thank you," he whispered.

The sound of his deep masculine voice frightened her and suddenly she realized the danger she'd put herself in by releasing him from his bonds.

At best, when they were tethered and on their penis leashes, males were unpredictable creatures. Untethered, they were rapists and killers, as last year's Slave Uprising had proven.

In her haste to get to the male, she hadn't thought of her safety. Hadn't thought of anything but capturing him.

She struggled to push aside her fear. She needed to keep her focus. Needed to stick to the plan. Needed to calm down.

"Quickly. You must stand so we can leave."

He nodded weakly and moved carefully as he struggled to his feet. He took one step forward and buckled to his knees, a hot curse on his lips.

Virgin stiffened at the outburst, half expecting the young women to hear his outcry and come running into the hide-house. The laughter outside continued and Virgin exhaled a sigh of relief.

"What's the matter?" she asked.

"Just give me a minute."

With her heart pounding violently in her ears, Virgin kept a watch on the door, hoping one or all of the women didn't notice that their passion-infected male was now loose.

"Ready," he whispered.

"Follow me." Virgin stepped through the rip she'd cut in the back wall to gain entrance to the shelter.

The male stumbled after her. His breathing sounded too harsh, his face was too pale in the early morning moon-glow.

Instinctively she knew he was hurting more than he was letting on.

Had she made a mistake rescuing him? Was he going to get her recaptured and sent back to prison and back to those fucking machines?

Not if she could help it.

Slipping her hand against his hot palm, she firmly pulled her new captive into the surrounding forest.

*****

They ran for what seemed an eternity, but Virgin figured it must have only been twenty or so minutes since she'd stolen him from the Yellow Hairs.

He held tightly to her hand as she led him through the dense forest. So tightly that she could feel every searing inch of his hot fingers interwoven with hers. He possessed long fingers and a strong hand. Strong enough that he could crush her bones if he'd a mind to do it.

For an instant she was paralyzed once again by fear for her safety, but the terror quickly turned to concern.

Sweat drenched his entire body. His skin was pale, his breathing labored.

Virgin frowned. It irritated her that she should feel sympathy for her captive. But she couldn't help it. He was a prize that would make her dream come true and she would do anything to ensure he stayed alive.

At the next small meadow they encountered she called a halt. He didn't waste any time plopping onto a nearby fallen log, dragging her down beside him.

While he rested, Virgin listened intently for indications that they were being followed. She heard nothing except his harsh gasps.

His shoulders shuddered heavily with every breath. Damp wisps of golden-brown hair drooped over a perfectly shaped forehead, hiding his eyebrows from her view. Dark lashes framed his tightly closed eyes.

A dark shadow of bristle covered parts of his face giving him a dangerous appeal. His nose was not too short, not too long. His nostrils flared wildly as if he were a stallion who'd just spent hours fucking his mares.

She fully understood why the male panted frantically. In its initial stages, passion poison sapped energy from all body parts, slowly drawing it to the sexual centers. Soon he would enter the second phase where he would feel a renewed strength but it would be centered on sex, not escape.

The signs of the oncoming second phase were already there—the pale glow to his skin, the erratic pounding of his pulse in his thick-corded neck and the frantic panting.

Her gaze dropped to the sparkling droplets of sweat glistening in his golden-brown chest hairs. How would that hair feel beneath her fingertips as she slid her hands over his hot, sweaty flesh?

Following the fine dusting that arrowed down the middle of his flat stomach, Virgin locked her eyes to the area between his widespread legs and to the most beautiful set of balls she'd ever seen.

They were perfectly shaped. Big. Hard looking. She couldn't stop her mouth from watering at the seductive sight.

That's when she noticed the cock ring practically strangling his pulsing penis. He wouldn't be able to travel fast until that problem was quickly taken care of. And there was only one way she could think of to get that cock ring off him.

"What are you doing?" the male cautiously asked as she dragged her knife from the scabbard.

His eyes were a magnificent green-blue and full of lust which encouraged a sweet flutter to scream through her belly. Her unwanted reaction toward him irritated her.

"That!" she snapped and pointed her knife at his erect cock, "has got to go."

He cursed and turned himself from her view.

Anger flashed hard and bright at his gesture. All males were trained to allow a woman to do whatever they wanted to them and it was illegal for males to shield their sex under any circumstances.

His cheeks darkened with a sexy blush and her anger disintegrated. She'd never seen a male who was embarrassed by a woman seeing his sex. His reaction was odd yet amusing.

Keeping his broad back toward her, he suddenly thrust out his hand. "Give me the knife; I'll take care of it."

"I don't think so!"

"What is the problem?"

"I'm not giving you a knife."

"What? You don't trust me?" His voice was coated with disbelief.

"Not on your life."

"It'll be both our lives if you don't give me the knife, 'cause I'm not letting you near me with it."

Virgin shook her head in despair. She'd never thought she would ever see the day when she would have to argue with a male. It was ridiculous. And frustrating.

Now she understood why women preferred not to educate them.

"Either you let me cut it off or I'm leaving you behind," she warned.

"You cutting *it* off is what I'm afraid of."

"I'm very efficient with a knife."

"I'm sure you are, lady, but I don't take chances where my body parts are concerned."

He wiggled his fingers impatiently, obviously still expecting her to give him her weapon.

"The knife stays with me, male. You will just have to trust me."

The way his magnificent shoulders sagged made Virgin realize she'd won the argument.

The male didn't so much as move a muscle, but eyed her with deep suspicion as she slid the handle of her knife tightly between her teeth and crouched in front of him.

Gently she grabbed his knees and pried his legs wide open to her.

Her eyes widened with appreciation.

What an exquisite size!

So unbelievably long!

His cock was so engorged it was a strange hue of purple. And it pulsed wildly as she stared at it.

She found herself licking her lips at the thought of having a taste of his fierce-looking shaft.

"Anytime, lady," his growl broke into her thoughts, forcing her to concentrate on the task at hand.

The way the thick ring was wrapped so tightly around his cock and balls she knew immediately if she dared use the knife she would certainly cut into this fine specimen.

But it was the only way to free him.

Or was it?

She swallowed at the realization there was another way.

But she couldn't do that!

Could she?

Shaking the lusty thoughts away, she angled the knife closer to his cock.

"Forget it," he hissed between clenched teeth.

"You cannot travel in this condition."

"I'll manage."

"The passion poison can protect your sex for only so long. I think you're already experiencing too much pain to wait any longer. It must come off. Now."

The way he frowned she knew he was thinking over what she'd just said.

"I cannot afford to get caught," she continued. "I will do what I think is best."

"Don't use the knife." His voice sounded strangled and…aroused?

Virgin blew out a shaky breath and tried to still her own excitement as it shifted like a bursting wave throughout her system.

She'd never hungered to suck on a male's cock before, but she sincerely desired to taste this one.

His lust-filled eyes lifted to peer at her and a shiver of pleasure zipped through her lower abdomen.

"I can do it myself. With my hands," he whispered.

She could tell by the sexual hunger shimmering in his eyes that he was struggling to keep his thoughts coherent. If she didn't hurry, Phase Two would grab hold of him and she wanted to have him secured in her shelter before that happened.

"It will take too long." Virgin found herself saying, fascinated by the realization she would be disappointed if she couldn't taste him.

Without another thought, she removed the quiver of arrows and bow she'd slung over her shoulder and placed it and the knife on the ground behind her.

Holding her breath she reached up to cup his enlarged sperm-laden balls.

He groaned softly as she tested their weight. His balls were so unbelievably heavy, so deliciously silky and hard.

With her heart thumping wildly against her chest she uncupped him and reached for the base of his swollen member.

The instant she touched him, his cock twitched and jerked. He was so immense. So unbelievably thick.

His desire-engorged cock stuck straight out at her. Purple with arousal, the enlarged plum-shaped head looked angry and begged to be suckled and comforted. A drop of seminal fluid oozed from the slit.

Resisting her excitement no longer, Virgin lowered her head. With her lips, she sensually traced the tip of his bulging cock as if she were applying lip balm.

Another groan, louder than the last, escaped his mouth.

She sent him a warning look to remain quiet but his eyes were already scrunched tight with pleasure. The muscles in his cheeks twitched as he clenched his mouth. Obviously he'd realized making noise at this point was not a safe option. But could he remain quiet for long with the passion poison raging through his system?

Her tongue tentatively swirled around the tip of his fierce thickness as she tested his resolve.

Another low growl crept up from somewhere deep in his chest. It was a primitive sound, a fierce noise that made a shimmering warmth shoot through her veins. Made a wetness accumulate between her legs.

The skin surrounding his cock felt satiny against her tongue. Beneath it his flesh felt oh, so deliciously hard.

She nipped her teeth against his flesh, aching to taste him. A dark growl struggled to escape his mouth. She backed off and once again swirled her tongue against the pulsing head, savoring the tang of male. She began to lick his swollen member in wide teasing stripes from tip to base, along his corded ridge from the underside.

Pressing her hands tighter around the base of his cock, she enjoyed the iron-hard strength of his pulsing member. Using the tip of her tongue she dug gently into the tiny slit in the head of his cock, sipping more of the pungent pre-come that slowly oozed out.

He moaned erotically and eased his legs further apart, allowing her to snuggle closer. Gently she pushed against his heated testicles hoping to ignite a release but at the same time hoping he wouldn't come so she could explore her own awakening, sexually starved body.

Her nipples had tightened into aching knots and warm liquid seeped along her inner thighs. And she experienced the overwhelming urge of wanting his heated length buried deep inside her cunt.

Suddenly his hands speared through her hair. Holding tight to both sides of her head he shoved his cock further into her open mouth.

The male was so huge he hit the back of her throat! And there was still more to come! The foreign hot cock in her mouth panicked her and she thought she might choke.

Thankfully he pulled back a bit and hissed between his teeth.

"Quit teasing. Just do what needs to be done, before I lose control."

Unfortunately the male had already lost control as he pulled himself out, bucked his hips forward and shoved more of his engorged flesh into her.

His immense size filled her mouth. His heat branded her and she instinctively tightened her lips around his slippery swollen flesh.

A pulse beat like a second heart along the length of him. His male odor was hot and musky. Sexy.

She sucked hard, drawing his rod deeper.

Thrusting his hips forward, he began to pump. His shaft slammed into her mouth and hit her throat again. She thought she'd gag at this unfamiliar action but then he withdrew quickly. She forced herself to relax her throat muscles and she welcomed him back in.

In and out he thrust.

She increased the pressure of her lips around his hot flesh, enjoying his erotic groans.

His male sounds were arousing to say the least. And to have a male ramming his ferocious flesh into her throat, fucking her mouth, was something brewed only in her wildest fantasies.

She loved it!

Loved sucking his cock. Feeling the strength of his rod. Loved the taste of him, enjoyed the idea that right at this moment, as he held her head firmly between his powerful hands, she was his slave.

Suddenly his hands tightened on either side of her head and she tasted more of the salty residue on her tongue. The male flavor made her cunt muscles contract wonderfully.

She found herself whimpering in shock at the pleasant sensations spreading deep in her womb.

Without warning his cock jerked wildly in her mouth and suddenly his hot seed shot down her throat.

She swallowed quickly, her lips tightening around him, milking him as fast and as hard as she could.

The male groaned again. It was a strangled cry. A sinfully arousing sound that unleashed a strange happiness inside her making her proud that she could bring him such pleasure. She knew for certain she wanted to hear that guttural sound again. But his cry was too loud and she hoped no one was close enough to hear.

She continued to suckle him, not that she had much choice with his hands holding her head captive. Instinctively she knew even if her head wasn't being held, she would still enjoy his heated flesh and the salty taste of his cock's release.

Finally he let go of her, pulling his limp rod out so quickly, he crashed back off the log, landing butt first onto the ground.

Their heavy breaths shot through the air like mini-explosions and Virgin's mind reeled at what she'd just done. She'd occasionally seen a Yellow Hair do this to the male slaves during a Virgin Dance, but she'd certainly never had the urge to do it herself, until now. And it had been a magnificent experience to say the least.

After she'd calmed somewhat, Virgin scrambled to her knees and, leaning over the log, reached between the male's legs. She needed to untangle the cock ring before the passion poison would have a chance to swell him up again.

But before she could touch him, his hand snapped around her wrist like a metal restraint, stopping her cold.

"I'll do it." Anger sparked his words. Confusion raged in his eyes. Confusion and something else. Regret?

Did she not do a good enough job in pleasuring him?

Oh! Why should she even care?

She'd done what needed doing and there was plenty more to come whether he liked it or not.

He released her wrist and frowned. "I'm sorry. I didn't mean to offend you. It's just that...I'm not used to...what just happened. I can't seem to control myself."

Well, join the club.

Without another word he worked on removing the cock ring. The raw whip marks covering his wide shoulders sent another unwanted sting of sympathy zipping through her.

The passion poison should have deadened the pain by now, she thought as she fought off the unwanted sympathy. And now that he'd had his first sexual release, the passion poison would become even more powerful. It wouldn't be long before his mind would cloud to any semblance of reason.

All he would think about was having sex.

Virgin couldn't stop her pulse from quickening at that thought.

She remembered all the Virgin Dances she'd had to witness as a Queen and then as a High Queen. Remembered when she was a young Yellow Hair she'd wanted so much to participate with the rituals like all her friends had done, yet her other priorities had kept her from doing so. Only virgins were allowed to become Queens and High Queens and so she'd focused on that instead of simply getting sexual release by fucking males.

She was promptly ripped from her thoughts when the air was split by the faraway war cries of the Yellow Hairs.

The familiar sound sent a frisson of fear slamming into Virgin. The Yellow Hair virgins had discovered the male missing.

That meant one thing.

The hunt for them was on.

Chapter Three

Aside from the first war cries they'd heard earlier, no other sound had erupted. Perhaps the virgins were busy tracking them? Or perhaps they'd decided to let the male go and find another one?

No. They would try and track him for a little while.

However she doubted the Yellow Hairs would pick up their trail. The virgins were too inexperienced. Even the elders wouldn't find her. Her few months of training as a High Queen had taught her the ultimate in stalking prey and covering up her tracks.

Up until an hour ago when she'd given the male relief with her mouth, she hadn't bothered covering their tracks. She'd wanted them to be followed. She'd led their trail directly to the river where she and the male had entered and gone downstream for about a mile. That's where the stream had split into two and where Virgin veered and took the left river. A few minutes later the river once again split, this time to three streams. The one she'd picked would split yet again just up ahead.

It would take their pursuers weeks to cover the territory. She felt relatively sure that wouldn't happen because the virgins would be eager to find another male, and it was well-known that the escaped sex slaves from last year's Slave Uprising had fled to The Outer Limits, not around here.

"I guess I should thank you for saving my life," the male huffed from behind her as they trudged through the waist-deep stream.

"No need. I was in the area." Which was the truth. She'd purposely ventured close to the Yellow Hair's secluded training camp hoping to hear tidbits of any news about her recent prison escape and had been quite thrilled to learn the virgins had captured a talking male.

"I was thinking, maybe now would be a good time for us to part company."

"No!" Virgin shouted as she whirled around to face him.

"No?" His eyes widened with surprise at her sudden outburst.

"I mean do you have any idea where you are?"

"No, but I'm sure I can find a way out of here." The sound of his voice wasn't confident at all. And the anxious look creasing his face made her realize he was worried. Probably upset with his body's rising uncontrollable sexual needs.

"There is no need to be afraid. The sexual urges you are feeling are due to the passion poison."

She was surprised yet again to see the red flush of embarrassment sweep across his cheeks.

"You'll need an antidote," she continued. "I can administer it back at my shelter."

"Maybe it would be better if you just tell me what this passion poison is made of and I can whip up an antidote. I think it might be safer for you if I wasn't near you."

The male was concerned for her safety?

How very interesting.

Every time she'd witnessed a male being infected with the passion poison he'd never been the least bit interested in protecting a female from harm. He'd only been interested in fucking as many as he could get his hands on.

And that was one of the purposes of the passion poison. With so few males around, the poison was administered in order to arouse the male for a long period of time without him tiring.

Perhaps because this male was a talking male he understood what was happening to him? If that was the case, his mind would be able to hold off on his sexual urges longer than an uneducated slave.

Virgin frowned.

What if he was so educated that she wasn't able to get him to submit to what she needed him to do to her?

If she couldn't cure him, her plan was dead.

"There's no time to explain about the ingredients in passion poison. It's much too complicated. However you still have time. There is a window of opportunity before you reach the point of no return."

His eyes narrowed with nervousness. "Point of no return?"

"It happens in Phase Four. The antidote takes twenty-four hours to administer. If it isn't administered by Phase Four you will die."

His Adam's apple bobbed fiercely as he swallowed. "How long before I reach this Phase Four?"

"Depends on your metabolism. If you have a fast one, it'll come quicker. I've seen males enter Phase Four as soon as ten hours after being poisoned unless the antidote was started."

"How long have we been running?"

"Four to five hours. You were infected two hours before we escaped."

"That leaves me with three to five hours. How far to your place?"

"A few more minutes."

"Well let's get moving. I need that antidote."

He passed her and trudged quickly through the waist-deep waters. She stared at the nicely rounded contours of his ass shimmering beneath the clear water and couldn't help but smile.

He certainly was a magnificent specimen of a male and obviously his energy was coming back.

He was moving easier. Sweat still drenched his yummy-looking body but it wasn't pouring off him anymore. His breathing wasn't harsh anymore either. That meant the male's system was preparing itself to enter Phase Two.

Virgin couldn't help but shudder with both excitement and dread at the thought of what would be coming next.

Phase Two meant his mental state would deteriorate and all he would think about was sex.

* * * * *

Buck couldn't seem to walk straight. Maybe the slippery river rocks beneath his bare feet had something to do with it but he didn't think that was the main reason. He couldn't think straight either. All he could concentrate on was the woman who'd rescued him.

Even now, as she waded along the stream in front of him, he couldn't stop himself from watching the seductive sway of her curvy hips tucked beneath that teasing piece of flimsy material. It was worse than if she'd been naked. At least then his curiosity wouldn't have been so piqued.

He inhaled a deep breath. Her fragrance caressed his senses until all he could think about was the fantastic blowjob she'd given him.

He'd never been so embarrassed, not to mention so aroused, in his damned life than when her velvety lips had curled around his cock like a scorching brand. The beautiful sight of her crouched between his widespread legs, the seductive licks of her burning tongue sliding up and down his rigid member and around his swollen shaft had sent screams of passion zinging through every nerve and fiber, every muscle and every brain cell.

He'd completely lost himself in the sensual cravings. His hips had bucked against her in a dangerous dance. His mind had swum in a haze of dark passion. And all thoughts of self-control had simply vanished.

She'd suckled so perfectly that he wondered how many times she'd sucked a cock before. A tremor of anger zipped through him at the thought of another man's hands roaming along the seductive contours of her velvety flesh. If he ever caught another man in her arms he'd rip the son of a bitch to shreds.

Buck blinked in shock at his hostile thoughts.

It had to be the passion poison talking. It had to be!

He wasn't normally the jealous type or a sex maniac but the way he was feeling since he'd been injected with the poison sure made him feel like he was both.

His self-control was disintegrating fast. He needed to concentrate on something else. Needed to place one foot in front of the other instead of thinking about grabbing her by her silky looking shoulders, pushing her down onto the sandy river bank, ripping those flimsy clothes off her and fucking her senseless.

Instinctively he knew if he concentrated hard enough, he could stop himself from taking her.

But how long could he hold out before his sexual urges became stronger than his self-control and he took her against her will?

The way his cock ached like a son of a bitch, it was only a matter of time.

Sooner rather than later.

With each step his self-control slid further away.

With each step he realized he loved the way her body moved. Loved the way her arms glided as she balanced herself with confidence on the slippery rocks in the warm stream. He couldn't stop himself from imagining the silky feel of her long legs wrapped around his hips as he made love to her.

Couldn't…

"We're here," she said softly, breaking into his searing thoughts.

Buck smiled in relief at the sight of the small storybook cottage partially camouflaged beneath a pile of green ivy and shaded by a few huge tamarack trees.

From here the only way he could tell it was a building was due to the gray wood-planked shutters caressing a small leaded window peeking through the green vines.

"Great hideout," he said as he followed her, his horniness momentarily subdued.

"It used to belong to the priestesses. They used it for their priestesses-in-training when they went on a spiritual retreat. It is abandoned during the stormy season which will start soon. No one is using it now. We will be safe here."

As he got closer, more details emerged. Beneath the trailing of hearty ivy, he noted a twin peaked roof. The middle sagged like an old horse's back and the irregularly-shaped gray roof shingles were carved from wood.

He was most impressed by the arched door, possibly made from red cedar. Braced by thick black iron hinges, it creaked slightly as Virgin opened it.

The coolness of the interior washed against his burning flesh. It was a one-room cottage decorated with only the basics, a rough wooden counter with an odd-looking hand pump that dripped water, a table and chairs in the middle of the room. The walls were gray stone boulders and the floor wood-planked.

He inhaled sharply the instant his gaze fell upon the narrow cot tucked in the corner. Visions of him throwing her onto the bed and plunging deep into her very depths shot new bursts of arousal through his entire body.

"Are you okay?"

He blinked at the sexy tone of her voice. She'd moved closer and her body heat wrapped around him like a seductive blanket. He gritted his teeth in frustration and swallowed hard, fighting the need to fuck her.

"The passion poison is getting stronger isn't it?" she asked.

"So, where's the antidote? You said it was in the cabin."

"It is."

Suddenly she looked shy. Nervous. Cuter than sin.

Shit! Even if he hadn't been infected, he would have seen she was one sexy gal.

Another thing he noticed too—she wanted to get laid.

He could read the lust in her eyes. Had sensed her needs when her eager lips had wrapped around his cock.

Breaking his gaze, she headed toward a back door.

"Where are you going?"

"Getting something to freshen us up."

Buck nodded in agreement. Heck, he needed something cold all right.

An ice-cold shower.

An ice-cold beer.

And a real long fucking session with the blonde beauty.

* * * * *

The instant Virgin closed the back door, she slumped against it, squeezed her eyes shut and shook her head.

Mixed emotions cascaded over her. One instant she was confident she could administer the cure; the next second panic and doubt assailed her.

A sob wrenched at her throat.

She didn't think she could bring herself to mate with the male. Even if fucking him would save his life.

Yet saving his life meant she would be able to use him to better her own current dismal conditions.

What a dilemma!

She had been a High Queen, for Goddess sake! It was forbidden for her to lie with a male. But if she didn't, he would die and her plans would die right along with him.

She squared her shoulders with defiance. She would not desert her plans under any circumstances. She would do what needed to be done. Nothing else at this moment was more important than keeping this male alive.

But first she needed to re-hydrate him in order to give him much needed energy. And she knew just the thing that would do the trick.

Plodding a few feet through the thick undergrowth, being extra careful to make sure no branches or twigs were disturbed, Virgin quickly found the sinkhole and drew a watermelon from the water.

He would appreciate the coolness of this feast before she seduced him. And it would give her a little extra time to gain her confidence at doing such a monumental task.

Quickly she headed back into the shelter. And froze.

The male lay on her cot, his sex hidden beneath a sheet, his eyes closed.

Alarm raced up Virgin's spine. If the male fell asleep again before she could begin to administer the cure he might never awaken. Unfortunately it was one of the down sides to the passion poison.

In a few quick strides, she reached his side.

Heart crashing in her ears, she leaned over him and pulled off the sheet. His heavily veined cock pulsed with arousal as she kissed the tip of his heated length.

He groaned. His eyes flickered open. Dangerous lust haunted his blue-green depths.

Excitement and fear bombarded her as she realized he'd entered Phase Two.

Without warning, he grabbed her wrist pulling her down on top of him.

Her breath caught at the fierce heat of his hard, damp body beneath hers. Grasping her chin with his thumb and forefinger he brought her face toward his. His lips neared hers, his warm breath promising good things to come.

Perspiration beaded his temples and the dark passion in his eyes mesmerized her. Made her tingle with an unknown need she found irresistible.

"You're so beautiful. So damned sexy. I can't keep my hands off you."

His words shocked her. Left her dazed. She'd never heard a male say such things to a woman. Never expected she'd enjoy hearing them.

Without warning, his mouth touched hers. He tasted of violent desires and erotic shocks as his magical mouth slid against her lips. Her cunt twisted sharp and sweet beneath his assault.

The unexpected heated sexual awareness made her head spin.

Images erupted. Visions of the violent way his swollen cock had thrust in and out of her eager mouth, the vein-riddled spear she suddenly craved to have buried deep within her vagina.

His large hands slid down her sides in one erotic line of fire making her melt beneath his touch. Her breasts felt fuller, her nipples tingled as they scraped against the thin material of her top and then flattened against the hard bands of muscles across his damp chest.

Suddenly his hands cupped her ass and he pressed her tightly against his body. The length of his inflamed cock sizzled like a brand against the naked flesh of her inner thighs. She found herself widening her legs in an attempt to straddle his powerful hips.

Opening her mouth, his tongue, brutal and swift, forced its way past her teeth, touching her with long sure strokes that ignited a magnificent blade of lightning between her thighs.

She'd never felt this way in her entire life.

Suddenly she was drowning. Dragged under by a current of carnal pleasure she couldn't get out of. Didn't want to get out of.

She wanted this male.

She wanted him now.

When she reached down to grab his cock, the male's hands clamped around her wrists, holding her hands captive. Slowly he lifted her arms over her head and using one hand, he held her wrists tightly there.

Unable to move her hands, Virgin felt a surge of panic.

Was she doing the right thing allowing the male full rein?

Passion poison was dangerous even with the gentlest of males and the fierce way his lips were roving all over her mouth showed he wasn't a gentle male.

A large hand slid seductively between their bellies, slipping into her shorts. The instant his hot thumb slammed against her clitoris she bolted. An eager finger slid erotically over her swollen flesh, creating a fantastic chafing that sent spirals of pure enjoyment ripping deep inside her.

Oh Goddess of Freedom!

Could this be what she'd been missing while she'd dedicated her life to being a High Queen and vowing never to lay with a male? Could this be what she'd given up so she could better the lives of other women? Women who didn't even want her help?

Women who themselves were enjoying the pleasures of males.

His mouth drew away and he buried his bristly cheek into the sensitive area between her shoulder and her neck.

"What the hell is happening to me?" his tormented cry shot straight into Virgin's heart. Guilt sifted through her excruciating pleasure.

"It's the passion poison," she explained. "Just give in to it. Fuck me."

"Are you sure you want this?" His voice was restrained, barely audible.

He needed to fuck her to live.

She needed him alive to carry out her plan.

"Yes," she whispered.

A finger slid deep into her cunt and Virgin jolted at the wonderful intrusion.

This was the first time she'd been intimate with a male. The first time a male's finger had ever been inside her.

And it felt so good.

Unbelievably delicious.

Another finger impaled her drenched channel and Virgin trembled beneath him.

"You're so wet. So ready," he whispered. "I have to look at you."

Within a blink of an eye he pushed her off him and got up.

Yanking her to her weak legs, he quickly shoved her to the table set in the middle of the room. His lusty gaze sparkled with such intense heat she almost cried out from the pleasure it created deep within her.

"On the table," he growled into her ear.

She didn't even have a chance to question what he was saying when his large hands cupped her ass cheeks. His fingers dug into her flesh as he lifted her off her feet in one swift motion and plopped her down on top of the table.

Confident fingers slid beneath her waistband. Swiftly he pulled her garment down her legs and off. Grabbing her ankles he lifted them high, spread them wide apart and placed her feet firmly against his hot muscular shoulders. Cool air hit her clit with such a wonderful caress she cried out from the seductive impact.

Her eyes widened with shock and her vaginal muscles spasmed with excitement as he steered his pulsing male flesh straight toward the juncture of her legs.

His cock seemed even bigger now. Bigger and longer than she'd ever seen it.

He was going to impale her with that!

A momentary pang of terror once again gripped her until she remembered why she was allowing him free rein.

Grasping the edges of the table with her fingers, she held on for dear life.

The mad lust in his eyes subsided briefly as he fought the effects of the passion poison. It frightened her to know he was so powerful. At the same time, it excited her. His pent-up passion would be so potent when he finally released it.

And he would release control. Eventually all passion-infected males did.

"Don't be afraid. Please, don't be afraid," he chanted.

"I'm not scared," she lied and found herself chanting the words along with him.

His long fingers gripped the base of his solid erection and he slowly moved his engorged cock between her legs.

She was terrified. And so excited she couldn't even think straight.

"I need to be inside you so bad. I need to fuck you so bad. I can't stop myself anymore."

"I'm not asking you to stop," she whispered, trying to ease the anguish bruising his face.

He aimed the bulging tip of his cock at her cunt opening. Her desperate grasp on the sides of the table increased as his thick head sliced her labia lips apart.

Beneath her right foot, his powerful shoulder muscles flexed violently as his right hand settled between her legs and his thumb massaged her puffed-up clitoris.

Oh yes! What a wonderful feeling.

Warmth pooled in her belly. Moisture seeped from between her widespread legs and her pleasure mounted until she couldn't help but gasp with delight.

Lifting her head, she found his eyes dark and glazed as he hesitated. His jaws were clenched tightly. A vein throbbed violently in his neck.

He was still fighting the passion poison. Still trying to hold himself back. Trying hard not to hurt her.

"Fuck me, please," she urged, wanting to be penetrated. Suddenly aching to feel his long cock buried inside her.

At the sound of her voice, his willpower ebbed away and with surprisingly careful restraint, he sunk his throbbing male flesh into her channel.

The tremendous pressure made her vaginal muscles scramble frantically to accommodate his monstrous size. Yet the silky way his thumb continued to seduce her clit encouraged more moisture to soften the way.

His shaft was hard, searing hot and oh, so long. In silence, she endured the pressure, the unbelievable fullness and watched in stunned fascination as his massive flesh slowly disappeared inside her.

It was the most erotic sight she'd ever seen.

His breathing grew harder and rougher as her vaginal muscles clenched around him like a second skin.

"Oh man, you feel so unbelievably beautiful," he ground out.

He withdrew slowly and then plunged into her warm channel with one solid thrust, impaling her.

Fire raged throughout as her insides seized his thick intrusion, throwing her immediately into a climax. It slammed into her with such a mind-sucking force, she could do nothing but throw her head back and gasp at the brutal waves washing over her.

The pleasure was unbelievable!

Her eyes squeezed tight. Heated blood roared in her ears.

He continued to thrust his hard shaft in and out of her in fast steady strokes. Every thrust smothered her with more pleasure. Flooded her with a desire she'd never known before. A desire to have this male's rod drive deeper into her.

Deeper. Faster.

"Harder," she groaned.

Instantly he obeyed. His strokes became harder, ruthless, more demanding.

Breathtaking pleasure slammed through her and she came violently. He continued to slide in and out of her cunt. Taking her harder with each and every stroke. Sucking sounds rent the air as he continued to mate with her. Plunging his cock in and out until she cried out from the beautiful orgasms crashing over her.

Finally his shaft stiffened inside her and a torrent of his white-hot liquid shot deep into her womb. Her cunt muscles spasmed yet again and she milked him mightily of his seed.

Chapter Four

Buck winced as her sharp nails dug painfully into his shoulders urging him not to withdraw his shaft from her sweet wet channel.

"Don't," she whispered.

At the sound of her softly spoken words, guilt slammed into him making his cheeks flame with embarrassment.

Oh man. What had he done?

He'd actually lost control of his senses. Fucked a beautiful stranger.

"I'm sorry. I shouldn't have done this to you. Everything is happening too fast. This isn't normal," he stammered.

"You needed to do it. It is the passion poison controlling you."

"That's no excuse. I should have left the instant you freed me. The instant I realized I was losing control whenever I looked at you."

He stared down between her legs, to where his cock lay buried deep inside her.

"And this is how I've repaid you."

Although he felt disgusted for losing control, seeing himself lodged inside her hot cavern made a shiver of erotic bliss zip through his body.

The pleasure frightened him. He'd never felt this way about a woman. Let alone a stranger, a woman who smelled of delicious sex. A woman who'd given him the best blowjob of his life, not to mention the best fuck he'd ever encountered.

And he wanted more from her. Much more.

He shook the sensual thoughts from his fogged brain.

"This is happening too fast. Way too fast. I have to leave." Having said that, he couldn't find the courage to dislodge himself from her warm pussy. It felt so damn right being inside her, so unbelievably perfect.

"It is too dangerous for you to leave."

"Why? You think we were followed?"

He gazed in alarm at the leaded window, expecting a shadow to be there, watching them.

Nothing moved.

"I haven't heard anything. I just want you to fuck me again."

Words every man wants to hear, but from a complete stranger?

"I really am wiped. Tired," he lied. Actually he felt great, quite ready to go at it with her again.

Her grip tightened over his shoulders. The desperation in her warm hands made him nervous. The fear in her eyes made him inhale sharply.

"What's wrong?" he asked slowly, not quite sure he wanted to know.

She inhaled deeply as if gathering her courage. Her luscious breasts heaved deliciously in front of him. Instantly his shaft hardened inside her.

So much for hoping he'd been miraculously cured from this passion poison. He'd never been able to get hard so soon after his release with other women. Obviously the drug was still very much alive in his system.

"I think it's time you gave me that antidote."

"I'm the antidote."

"What?" Surely she was joking.

"To the passion poison. I'm the antidote."

Buck blinked with disbelief, trying to figure out if she was kidding.

"Fucking is the antidote for passion poison," she explained. "Twenty-four hours of sex with brief rest periods."

Twenty-four hours!

Shock ripped through his insides. He'd never heard of such a thing. Fucking a woman would heal him?

"You're crazy!"

Before she could stop him, he withdrew his hard shaft from her sweet channel and pulled away.

"I can't believe I fell for this. There is no passion poison antidote, is there? You just wanted to use some poor sap to give you a good time. And I bloody well fell for it. You must be some sick, twisted nymphomaniac."

Even as he said it, he knew it wasn't true. She wasn't a nympho. He was the sicko. His massive erection proved it.

Panic prompted him to grab the sheet off the nearby bed. Twisting it around his waist, he covered himself, and then headed for the door.

"If you leave, you will die."

The firmness in her voice made Buck stop dead in his tracks.

"You feel well enough now," she continued. "But that will change soon."

"How so?"

"Right now the most prevalent sensation on your mind is having sex again, right?"

She was right. He was thinking about fucking her again. But damned if he was going to do it!

"Soon you will enter Phase Three. If we don't copulate during that phase—"

"Bull! If I'm infected with some sort of poison, my brothers will find the cure."

"There's no time. We have to mate again. You must follow your urges."

"This is ridiculous."

"If we don't have sex..."

"I'm not buying into this crap!" he snapped.

"Are you not aroused?"

Aroused was an understatement.

"Please stay."

"I have to leave." God, did he ever have to get out of here.

He took one step forward and stared at the door.

It was his escape hatch, a way to leave this insanity, a way to leave her. Call him stupid, but he couldn't quite bring himself to go out that door.

Oh man! He wanted her again. Wanted to sink his cock into her delicious warmth. To kiss her pretty pink lips and catch her gasps of arousal into his mouth.

"I will tell you everything about the passion poison. Then you will understand," she prodded.

Buck closed his eyes and cursed in defeat.

"Sit down. I will prepare something for you to eat. I'm sure you are very hungry. It is the end stage of Phase Two."

Hungry wasn't the word for it. He was famished. Famished for food.

And starved for a taste of that luscious feast waiting for him between her legs.

He turned around and jolted at her flushed cheeks, the sweet innocent look of need on her face.

Cripes! Was she infected with this stuff too? Is that why she wanted him to fuck her again?

He shook his head in despair and plopped into a nearby chair, making sure he kept the sheet tented over his now painful erection.

"Okay, tell me about this passion poison."

She headed to the scarred wooden counter nestled under a small square window. Reaching into a nearby cupboard, she dragged down a small wicker basket and started throwing different types of fruit into it.

"The passion flower grows in The Outer Limits. Every year a group of Yellow Hairs gets special permission from the High Queens to go out and gather it. The petals are taken from the flowers, ground and mixed with sweetened saltwater. Then other ingredients are added. Only a Priestess knows what those additional ingredients are."

"So I'll get some of this passion poison from these Yellow Hairs and the Priestess. Where can I find them?"

"You are a male. Or have you forgotten that fact? Males are not allowed to roam free. If anyone sees you, you will be hunted and caught immediately. You were extremely lucky with the Yellow Hair virgins. If it had been anyone else you had spoken to, you would have been dealt with quickly and harshly instead of slowly as the Yellow Hairs had planned."

Ah yes, those naked virgin blondes, or as she called them, Yellow Hairs. As if injecting him with poison wasn't harsh enough, Buck thought with distaste.

"There are two main reasons why passion poison is used exclusively on males who will be the vessel for the young Yellow Hair virgins into womanhood."

Those sweet young ladies with the whipping fetish were virgins? Gee, why was he not surprised?

"Before the Virgin Dance begins and while the male is unconscious the virgins collect the Sacred Drink from him."

Uneasiness slithered up his spine. "Sacred Drink?"

"Your semen."

Oh great. They'd jerked him off while he'd slept.

"Lovely tradition," he muttered.

"During the Dance the females cut themselves on their arms. They collect the entire group's blood and mix it with your semen. It's the Sacred Drink. Traditional for all Virgin Dances."

Enough information already.

"Okay. So tell me exactly how this poison works." Maybe he could find a cure if he knew how to stop it.

"It seeps quickly into your nervous system encouraging your body to relax. The body goes into shock and you fall asleep. At the same time, the secret herbs kick in making your nerve endings extremely aroused to someone's touch."

"I'd rather think it's a simple physical attraction between a man and a woman instead of a stupid flower," he muttered.

She smiled prettily as she plopped a bowl filled with food in front of him.

Buck couldn't help but notice the shapes of some of the fruits and vegetables. Phallic-looking, such as carrots, cucumbers, and bananas.

His heart rate soared at the sight of her lovely naked breasts and her plump burgundy nipples that must taste as sweet as ripe cherries.

The urge to take her into his arms was so great he almost did it. Instead, he dug his nails into his palms until a sharp pain sizzled there. To his shock, it quickly turned into a feeling of arousal.

Oh boy.

He needed another distraction.

He eyed the food-laden bowl. He'd eat. That's what he'd do. He'd eat to take his mind off her.

Grabbing a banana from the basket, he quickly peeled it and began to devour the sweet treat. As he chewed, he found himself watching her.

Oh man, she sure did look yummy all naked and available for him as she watched him eat.

"Why do these women poison their men? Why force a man to have sex with them? Can't they find their own guys?"

"Virgin Dances and passion poison are Yellow Hair traditions. The passion poison is administered to make the male sexually aroused and able to take on many females at the same time because there has always been a shortage of males. During a Virgin Dance, a single uninfected male cannot pleasure so many females at once. That is why the poison is administered. So he can perform for hours with many different females."

Instead of six, he had one. And she was already a handful.

"And the second reason?"

"To season the male's flesh for after the fucking ceremony."

Season the male? What the hell did she mean by that?

Suddenly he remembered mention of being killed. His neck corded in shock and he could feel the beginnings of a headache beating at the back of his head.

"You mean like they wanted to kill me and eat me?"

Virgin nodded.

"It's a tradition."

"Another charming custom," he said dryly.

At least she was telling him the truth about them wanting to kill him. That meant she was probably telling him the truth about everything else.

She genuinely wanted to cure him. And what a nice way to get cured.

Suddenly the sensual curves of her sweet hips seemed sweeter, her erotically shaped ass more inviting. He'd had a brief feel of those hot ass cheeks in the palms of his hands when he'd lifted her onto this very table.

It had all happened so fast. Way too fast.

He'd lain down on the bed with hopes of resting his eyes and calming his racing mind when her sexy feminine fragrance had drifted beneath his nostrils and her sensuous lips had kissed the tip of his throbbing shaft.

At that moment he'd wanted her more than anything else in the world.

And he'd taken her.

Buck grabbed a peach from the basket and bit into it.

"Exactly what can I expect next?"

"A mild headache, but that will diminish as your sexual desire increases."

Already happening.

"What else?"

"It depends," she said quietly.

"On?"

She bit her bottom lip self-consciously and her eyes darted away from his gaze. A pretty dark blush swept across her cheeks.

Suddenly he was very eager to hear what she had to say.

"Your secret fantasies. As you enter the next phase, you will become more sexually aggressive. You will feel an increased need to act out your deep sexual desires."

His deep sexual desires?

His throat went dry. Fear raced up his spine. Oh man. He was in big trouble. Or better put, she was in big trouble.

If he pursued his deepest darkest sexual desires he might hurt her. And the last thing he wanted to do was hurt the woman who was trying to save his life.

Maybe he should leave. Right now.

Buck inhaled a sharp breath as a new thought formed.

Maybe he should stay and live out those fantasies?

It was quite obvious by the sexy sparkle in her eyes she wanted another go with him. And if she didn't want to have sex again, she knew where the door was.

She moved closer to him. Her heady scent caressed his senses, making him wild. Urging him to touch her and wanting her touch.

"What is your name?" she asked softly.

"Buck. Buck Hero."

"My name is Virgin. Virgin Ellis."

"I need for you to tie me down, Virgin. I can't fight this and worry about your safety at the same time."

To his surprise she visibly shivered. Instinctively he knew it wasn't out of fear but out of arousal.

"Is that one of your dark fantasies? To be tied down?" she asked softly.

"Please, just do as I ask." Damned if he was going to admit he was actually looking forward to being tied down.

"I will do as you ask but I have to warn you, you won't be safe from me."

The seductive promise in her sweet voice made Buck's body blaze with a savage heat he needed to douse. It was an electrifying heat that frightened him. To his surprise, his fear shifted to arousal.

The passion poison was increasing in strength.

"Just hurry," he urged, feeling his control slipping by the second.

Placing his hand into hers, he hoped he knew what he was doing by giving her all his trust.

Chapter Five

The bindings holding Buck Hero's wrists and ankles as he lay nude on the bed were totally secure. That knowledge gave Virgin the encouragement to do what needed to be done. And, she secretly added to herself, something she wanted to do too.

Eagerly she carved the watermelon she'd retrieved earlier from the pond.

"I don't think that'll be good enough to cool me down this time around, Virgin," he called out.

"It's not meant to cool you down. It's meant to heat you up."

A soft curse followed.

She detected arousal in his voice but it was overshadowed with fear. A fear she was sure came with acknowledging the dark fantasies his poisoned mind was conjuring up. Secretly she was glad he'd come up with the idea for her to tie him down. There was no telling how sexually violent a male would get under the poison, and with his massive shaft he would surely have done some damage when he'd unleashed his fantasies upon her.

"Don't fight the passion poison anymore, Buck," she said as she placed the watermelon-filled basket on the small stand beside the bed. "You must give up full control and embrace it. I'll take care of the rest."

"I don't give up control that easily, Virgin. It's not in me."

"I'm afraid you don't have any choice in the matter."

Feminine power raged throughout her at the sexy sight of his nude body splayed out on the bed totally at her mercy.

Looking at the thick pulsing cock with the bulging purple head near to bursting between his splayed legs, made the marrow in her bones melt and heated blood roar through her ears. She was going to enjoy sexually torturing him. Enjoy teasing him until he lost the will to fight the poison and begged her to fuck him.

Suddenly she wanted to touch him. Smell him. Taste him.

She wanted to have sex with him. Wanted to impale herself on his cock. And she wanted to do it now!

"You like what you see?" His voice was thick and husky.

"You have a magnificent body," she whispered truthfully.

"Then untie me. Do it now before I explode. I want to make love to you. I want to make you scream with passion."

The lust in his eyes shone brighter at his last few words. She recognized the wild look taking hold of him. Phase Three had begun.

"Shh, good things come to those who wait," she whispered, trying to soothe him.

He groaned with frustration and the corded muscles in his arms bunched as he pulled against his restraints.

For a minute his eyes lost the glaze and he said quickly, "Whatever you do, don't cut me loose. No matter how much I beg. I want to do things to you, Virgin. Things that'll hurt you."

His words radiated a feral heat that shot hot fragments of arousal deep within her womb.

"Don't worry. Just feel the passion. Let yourself go."

His breath hitched as she feverishly slid her hands over the whip-scarred skin of his broad shoulders, her fingers tangling into the warm silky hair on his chest.

"I don't want you to be afraid, but I just can't control it anymore," he whispered.

"I've seen poisoned males many times before. I was a High Queen. I had to witness the couplings after the Virgin Dances. What you are experiencing is normal."

"So you've had your share of males." Disappointment etched his voice.

"High Queens are not allowed to lay with a male. They aren't supposed to need a mere male."

Goddess of Freedom! Forgive her but she needed this male. Needed him to fill the aching emptiness between her legs.

He tensed. "You were a virgin before I fucked you?"

"No. I've had other sexual experiences before you came along."

"How many?"

"Several, but not with a male."

"Females?" His glazed eyes blinked with curiosity.

"Let's not talk about me. Let's concentrate on getting you cured."

She slid his right nipple between her finger and thumb, rolling it roughly until she heard his breathing quicken.

"Does it feel good?"

"I can take anything you can dish out," he said with defiance.

She smiled at the challenge in his voice and slid a cool watermelon chunk over the nipple she'd just aroused.

"Feel good?"

"Like heaven."

"How's this feel?"

Leaning over, Virgin inhaled the sensual scent drifting off his body. He smelled of sweat, sex and male. It was a tantalizing combination that urged her to continue with her seduction.

She sucked his hard nipple into her mouth as if it were a succulent berry. It quivered as her tongue laved his areola, then she sank her teeth into his flesh.

He cursed beneath his breath.

The taste of his nipple in her mouth and the sexy sound of his thick voice unleashed a desperate need in her.

She let his nipple loose and placed a cool watermelon chunk over it.

Trailing light touches with her lips, she felt the bands of chest muscles ripple against her mouth and headed for his other nipple. Pushing aside the other chunk of watermelon she nipped his cool flesh.

He moaned again and her cunt muscles spasmed in response.

Sliding her mouth from his flesh, she trailed more feather-like touches up his damp hard chest, along the side of his hot neck, over his strong jawline and to his sensually curved lower lip.

He whimpered as she suckled at his mouth. His lips were soft and demanding. Blood pumped heated arousal through her veins. Her breasts tingled with the need to be squashed against his hard chest, yearned to be cupped by his large hands.

When he tried to force his tongue between her teeth she slipped away, replacing her mouth with her nipple.

He latched onto her like a starving male, his dangerous teeth nipping aggressively at her tender flesh. Virgin cried at the unexpected pleasure-pain searing through her breast and pulled away.

The teasing glint in his eyes made her inhale sharply.

"You going to fuck me or tease me all night?" he asked.

"I've only just begun my seduction, male," Virgin whispered as she grabbed another chunk of watermelon. Using the cool fruit, she caressed the burning bite on her throbbing nipple.

"Hurt?" he asked.

"A little."

"Give me your other one."

She hesitated. The lust darkened his eyes wonderfully and she knew the passion poison was once again working its magic on Buck Hero.

"You won't be sorry," he prodded. His breath grew raspier, louder. "I want to suckle your breasts, Virgin. I want to taste your flesh."

Mesmerized by the seductive tone of his voice, she found herself rubbing another cool chunk of watermelon on her untouched nipple before offering herself to him once again.

His mouth eagerly latched onto her nipple and she cried out as sharp teeth once again nipped at her tender flesh. This time she didn't draw away and allowed the pleasure-pain from the male's hot mouth to sift through her.

Grabbing another piece of watermelon she slid it to the area where the male's searing mouth clutched her nipple. Brushing it gently over his upper lip, she watched him suckle her breast.

Arching her back, she pushed herself closer against his head, relishing the expert way his teeth nipped painfully and quickly stoked the fire with his hot velvety tongue. A tongue that zipped out of his mouth and captured the juicy piece of fruit caressing his upper lip. With an expert swiftness, he sucked the watermelon into his mouth and pressed the cool flesh against her burning nipple.

She sighed as the delightful treat eased the fire. Soon however, the fruit grew warm and the male chewed it quickly.

"Your cunt," he whispered against her breast. "I want to taste your cunt."

Was he serious? The male wanted to taste her? Down there? She stared at his flushed face and knew he indeed spoke the truth.

She grew eager to experience the feel of his hot velvety tongue stroking her down there but first she wanted to try something new.

Heart pounding with excitement, she climbed upon the bed and straddled her feet to both sides of his head.

Bending over she grabbed a nice-sized wedge of watermelon from the basket and slid the fleshy part of it between her legs. She moaned softly as the cool treat sliced her pulsing labia lips apart.

Down below Buck emitted a dangerous growl. "Are you coming down here or are you putting on a tease?"

Virgin's pulses skittered at the heat shining in Buck's eyes. She wanted to feel his thick tongue plunge up inside her but she also wanted to tease him a little too.

"I'm having sex. I don't know about you," she said as she continued to glide the luscious watermelon slice back and forth against her quivering clit.

He cursed and squeezed his eyes shut as if he were suddenly in pain.

"You afraid you aren't up for a show?" Virgin challenged softly.

His eyes snapped open and he groaned.

"You're killing me here, Virgin," he complained.

"Die later, male."

She watched his eyes glaze with hunger as he stared up between her legs while she sawed the cool wedge back and forth in pleasing movements and ground her hips in a carnal teasing gesture showing off what he was missing.

Sticky wetness saturated her inner thighs as she rubbed the thick wedge in quicker movements. The coolness did little to stifle the burning lust growing between her legs. She could smell her arousal intermingle with the watermelon's sweet scent. Could hear her shallow whimpers. Felt the pleasure of an oncoming climax.

"Come down here. Come inside my mouth," the male urged, sensing what was happening to her.

Shifting the wedge of watermelon aside, she quickly squatted over his flushed face.

His long pink tongue flicked out and speared savagely against her swollen clit. It sent a sharp jolt of energy pooling hot and heavy inside her lower belly.

"You taste so unbelievably good," he chuckled from beneath her. "Sex and watermelon. Fantastic combination. We'll have to do it more often."

Before she could agree, his tongue fondled her labia lips, swirling magic circles around and over her woman's bud. Dangerous sensations threatened to consume her. She bit her lip in a desperate effort to stave off the oncoming climax. She wanted to hold onto this beauty for as long as she possibly could.

"I guess I'll have to work a little harder for my meal," he growled.

She whimpered as his mouth clamped over her clit. His lips drew her plump labia lips into his hot mouth. At the same time his tongue thrust deep into her moisture-slick vagina.

A dark, primal, lusty moan escaped her mouth as his thick tongue pulsed in and out of her wet pussy in teasing strokes as if it were a miniature cock.

Every muscle in her grew taut. Her heart raced. Her breasts bounced with each tortured breath.

His tongue thrusts became firmer.

Heat suffused her entire body. Her pussy clenched violently and a climax sizzled through her womb. It slammed into her hard, sucking her into an all-consuming release that had her gasping for air as it washed over her in a seductive haze.

Instinctively, she gyrated her hips, drawing herself deeper into the rewarding pleasure as his tongue pummeled her with ruthless strokes. Her vaginal muscles clenched violently around his tongue and she could literally feel herself flowing into his waiting mouth.

When the climax finally faded away, Virgin breathed deeply, her flushed body weakening. Pulling her trembling hips back she settled her ass on his heaving hot chest.

"You look so beautiful when you climax," he commented after a few moments.

Virgin opened her eyes and saw his lips were glistening brightly from her release. The sight of it made the familiar warmth spread through her belly again. Her mouth suddenly dry and her heart pounding up a storm, Virgin knew exactly what she wanted.

"I want your cock. I want it now," she breathed.

His pupils dilated with arousal and he answered with an animalistic growl. The loud sound sliced through her, making her shiver with want.

As she angled herself upward, she was now allowed full view of his lust-hardened purple shaft. It jerked wildly and Virgin blew out an aroused breath, suddenly anxious to be impaled.

"Dammit! I want you so bad too. I've never wanted a woman as bad as I want you," he whispered.

It was strange hearing those words said especially for her. It unleashed an odd happiness inside her heart.

Suddenly she wanted to bring him the same pleasures he'd given her, wanted to show him how much she enjoyed having sex with him.

Squatting down over his pelvis, Virgin hissed as his bulging head slid into her wet channel. She felt her vaginal muscles clench tightly around him. The erotic feeling of fullness weakened her and she let her legs crash beneath her, allowing his thick cock to sink furiously to her innermost core.

The instant his thick balls slammed against her flesh Virgin leaned forward, digging her fingers into his thickly muscled shoulders, eagerly accepting his violent upward thrusts.

She hummed with beautiful sensations and a climax built quickly.

Their unified cries and groans of pleasure split the air and pulsed around them as they both fought for their release. Perspiration dampened her skin. She stiffened as the orgasm quickly overwhelmed her. The odor of their sex flooded her nostrils and suddenly she wanted to feel his succulent mouth upon hers.

Bending herself forward, she brought them belly to belly. Her nipples scraped against his chest muscles and she attentively touched his hot lips with hers.

The male responded immediately. He took her mouth fiercely, sparking more pleasure throughout her vagina.

She tasted her come in his mouth. It made her heady with need.

With a renewed desperation she thrust her hips harder against his sleek body, lifting and then crashing down upon his swollen cock with a renewed burst of energy.

In response, the male groaned wickedly into her mouth. His eyes were now closed tightly. His heart pounded violently against her chest.

Her fantastic orgasm was long and convulsive, subsiding slowly to a dull roar, and she realized he kept pumping frantically upwards.

He had finally given up control to the passion poison. His violent bucking frightened her, but there was no pain as his long thick penis thrust in and out. There was only the beautiful fluttering of another orgasm as it built quickly deep inside her.

This climax hit her hard, harder than any previous ones.

She gasped into his mouth as the spirals of pleasure slammed over her. She gave into it. Gave up control.

All her tumultuous emotions cascaded around her in one bright waterfall of beautiful sensations. She wanted to cry. She wanted to laugh. She wanted to scream.

Her mind and body were shattering into a thousand blissful pieces and then suddenly all the emotions and sensations drew together into one magnificent spasm of pleasure that made her cry out shamelessly. Dimly she heard the male's hoarse shout as he unleashed his hot release deep into her woman's core.

* * * * *

The sweet soreness between Virgin's legs throbbed as she watched Buck Hero's sleeping naked figure with a growing affection. She'd never known a male could bring a woman so much pleasure. If she had, she might have considered giving up all the hard work she'd gone through to achieve Queen and High Queen status.

But in the end her status in the community was gone anyway. Now she was a fugitive. Freshly escaped from prison and on the run.

And she had an educated male on her hands. A male who was alive and almost cured. A male she could use for her own benefit.

She could now set her plan into motion. Yet she hesitated.

The thought of betraying him left a sour taste in her mouth.

But it was something she had to do. There was no other way.

Except for telling him the truth.

Virgin closed her eyes and shook her head.

There was a chance he would say no to helping her. And if he said yes and they couldn't come up with another plan, he'd leave and she'd lose her only bargaining chip.

Slinging her quiver of arrows and bow over her shoulder, she lifted the door latch and slipped out into the hot afternoon sunshine.

She took a step forward then stopped at the sound of rustling in the bushes about forty feet away.

Was someone there?

She went very still and listened intently.

The rattling in the bushes stopped abruptly and Virgin relaxed. She'd probably spooked a deer or a panther. They were always lurking around in the bushes and drinking from the nearby streams.

Besides no one knew about this hideout, except for the people who had helped her escape and they would never betray her by giving her away to the authorities. She had nothing to worry about.

At least not yet she thought when she spotted the dark ominous clouds stalking toward the mid-afternoon sun.

Her hand dropped to the hilt of the knife strapped to her thigh making sure it was easily accessible. If she needed it, she knew she wouldn't hesitate to use it. She also knew if she didn't leave now, she would never do what needed doing to get the ball rolling on her plan.

With a heavy heart and double-checking to make sure the coast was clear, Virgin slipped into the bushes and headed toward her mission of betraying Buck Hero.

Chapter Six

After following the stream to the rivers and then finally onto land, Virgin moved quickly. Overhead, thunder growled with a menacing sound. The sun had disappeared behind dark clouds and everything looked drab and bleak.

She felt the same way.

Her guts crunched up with guilt and pain at what she had decided to do. When she finally spied the gray stone prison in the gloom of the oncoming storm, she almost turned around.

Almost walked away.

Almost gave up on the idea of betraying Buck.

Almost gave up on her dream.

Then she spotted the guard standing at the door of the building and knew she had no other choice but to go through with her plan. If she waited until tomorrow to let them know about Buck, it might be too late. Crouching low, she inhaled a shuddering breath and prayed her courage would last.

Reaching behind her shoulder, she loosened an arrow from her quiver and placed it against her bowstring. Pulling the arrow back, Virgin aimed it at the guard's heart.

"I've come to see the prison warden!" she shouted from her hiding place.

The guard's hand slid quickly to the disintegration gun she wore at her right hip.

Virgin lifted the bow slightly and let loose an arrow.

It whizzed through the air and slammed hard into the bark of a nearby tree.

The guard stiffened the instant she realized she was in danger.

"Who speaks?" The guard called out.

"It's Virgin! I've come to see the prison warden. Bring her out. I have a deal to make with her.

The guard's lips curled into a wicked sneer that made Virgin inhale a frightened breath.

"The warden makes no deals with escaped convicts."

"She will with this one. Go fetch her. Get her out here within a minute or I leave. Tell her I'll make it worth her while."

The guard nodded and quickly disappeared inside the prison.

Tears rippled into Virgin's eyes as she waited. This wasn't at all how she'd planned on feeling.

She should be happy at being so close to ending her torment. Instead, she was crying like a baby.

Not even a minute passed when the door to the prison opened. To Virgin's uneasiness, Cath, the newly self-proclaimed Queen of the area, stepped outside.

Once again Virgin almost backed out of the plan.

Cath was a woman she shouldn't trust. But Virgin had come so far. She was so close to victory she could taste it. There was no other choice but to deal with Cath.

"Must be something very important to bring you back here, Virgin!" Cath shouted.

"I'm here to make a deal."

"I know what you want, Virgin, but I don't make deals with escaped convicts. You should know better than that."

Virgin swallowed hard trying desperately to get rid of the dry anxiety clogging up her throat. "I have one of the talking males."

Cath tried hard not to show it, but Virgin could see she was visibly shaken.

"Have I gotten your attention?"

Cath nodded and asked softly, "So? Where is he?"

"He is slightly injured. He will be ready to travel by tomorrow. You'll get him only if I get what I want…unharmed."

"I want the talking male now, Virgin. Tell me where he is and we'll go and get him. When I have him, I'll give you what you want."

The last thing Virgin could afford to do now was give away her secret hideout. She was going to need it over the upcoming stormy season.

"No. Either you agree to tomorrow or I walk away from this deal. You don't get what you want and I don't get what I want."

She held her breath and awaited Cath's answer. If Cath didn't agree, Virgin would most likely start screaming hysterically and maybe never stop.

"All right, Virgin. Bring him here tomorrow and you'll get what you want."

"Not here. I'll pick the place to meet."

"No. You bring him here. Tomorrow. Or the deal is off. Take it or leave it."

Before Virgin could protest, Cath turned and disappeared into the prison.

* * * * *

Virgin stumbled through the stream as cool rain poured over her heated body.

The sky had turned an ugly bruised gray and the howling wind blew her blonde hair into her eyes, eyes that blurred with tears of confusion.

She'd done it. She'd told Cath about Buck.

An arrow of guilt rippled up Virgin's spine at what Cath would do to him. She'd strap him to the fucking machines. Use his sperm to impregnate the female prisoners. Most likely program the sophisticated machine to pick only the sperm that contained the DNA for creating well-hung males.

Cath would be rich and she would put The Breeders, who were the only ones at the moment supplying the area with males, out of business.

Unfortunately, this time Virgin wouldn't be around with her secret remedies to stop the prison women from getting pregnant.

But at least she would be free to go wherever she wanted.

And she'd have her dream fulfilled.

That idea, however, wasn't as sweet as it once had been, not at what she would have to do to get it.

In the gloom of the storm she missed the shelter and had to track back over a half an hour.

The creak of the door hinges as she entered the shelter was dampened as a roar of thunder chased her quickly inside.

Rain drummed on the roof like a thousand fists and the wind shrieked against the tiny windows. She was relieved she was back safe and sound and very glad to have the male warming her bed.

"Where were you?" The male's warm voice curled out of the dusky corner where she'd left him.

"I went out for a walk," Virgin explained as she padded closer to him trying to figure out why suddenly the hairs on the back of her wet neck were bristling with warning. Something seemed different. She couldn't figure out if it was something with the male or something in the shelter, but something seemed out of place.

"That was one hell of a long walk," he chuckled.

Fire heated up her chilled body the instant she saw his eyes ablaze with arousal. However they weren't as bright as they'd once been, which meant fucking him was working against the passion poison. He was well on his way to being cured. But she still had some work to do.

"I wanted to let you sleep," she explained as she approached his magnificent body tangled in the sheets.

Quickly she flung the cover away revealing his nakedness to her. His perfectly shaped balls looked hard and near to bursting and his swollen vein-riddled cock jerked wonderfully beneath her appreciative gaze.

"How about you getting out of those wet clothes and letting me loose so we can pick up where we left off?"

His soft-spoken words drove away her uneasiness. She trembled with the familiar craving to have him furiously fucking her. It was the only time she didn't think about betraying him. The only time she didn't have to face reality.

She shook off the quiver of arrows from her shoulder and removed the knife and scabbard strapped to her leg. Slipping the soaked clothing from her she quickly worked the ropes that had secured him to the bed.

"You must have been pulling at these binds quite a bit. They seem looser," she said.

He didn't say anything and the instant he was free, he pulled her down until she laid full length on the narrow bed beside him. She snuggled against his hard lean body, grateful for the intense heat radiating off him and curling against her damp skin. The familiar primitive cravings to feel his engorged cock sliding into the aching emptiness between her legs suddenly erupted like an inferno.

"Have I told you how much I'm attracted to you? How much I'd really like to get to know you?"

Virgin closed her eyes to blind herself from the naked truth in his words. She didn't deserve his kindness or his sexual pleasure. And she certainly didn't deserve his trust. Not after what she'd just agreed to with the prison warden.

Propping his head on an elbow, he gazed at her as his fingers brushed away the wisps of rain-soaked hair plastered against her cheeks.

"I'd like that too," she found herself whispering, getting sucked into his fantasy, a fantasy that would never come true.

"You mentioned earlier that you'd had sexual relations but without a male. I was your first then?"

Her eyes snapped open at that question and she came face to face with an odd look brewing in his eyes. If she didn't know any better she'd say he was angry with her. Angry that he'd been her first? Or was it something else?

Outside, another snap of thunder crashed and she moved closer against Buck's hot body.

"You afraid of storms?" he asked softly. There was no sign of the earlier anger in his voice, only concern.

"I've never really been before."

"What's different now? Why are you so nervous?"

"I guess I'm just tired," she lied.

"Too much walking."

She nodded.

"You didn't answer my question about me being your first male."

"Yes, you are my first male."

His breath blew hot against her neck and she discovered his body melting against hers. How interesting that her answer relaxed him to such a degree.

"It's important that you are my first. Why?"

"I was just curious."

"Just curious?"

"Okay, so I wondered how I rated in the sex department."

Virgin smiled against the curve of his shoulder. The male wanted to know if he was any good sexually. Competition was a healthy reaction in males. She'd often watched the competitions in the Brothel Town when several eager males were instructed to lie down on the ground and the women would impale themselves on their stiff cocks, each trying to make their own male reach an orgasm first in order to win the contest.

"So? How was I?" His hot hand slid along her naked stomach and dipped seductively into her navel where he massaged in tiny erotic circles.

"Not bad," she gasped as arrows of fire streaked from her belly button straight into her womb.

Goddess! She hadn't known her belly button was such an amazing sex tool.

"Just not bad?"

"It's better than not good," she teased.

He was silent for a moment and then the long finger left her belly button and slid a trail of erotic fire over her abdomen. Her lower belly blazed and clenched beneath his hot touch.

His middle finger slipped between her eager thighs.

Liquid heat flared and immediately pooled there. She could hear the slurpy sounds as he slid his finger between her plump labia and rubbed her slippery, lust-engorged clitoris.

Her breaths grew shallow and she trembled wonderfully beneath his delicate touch.

"Is that better than not bad?" he growled against her ear.

She nodded eagerly, wanting more.

"I missed you when you were gone," he said. "I woke up a couple of times and it felt rotten not having you lying beside me. Not being able to reach out and gather you into my arms."

Oh Goddess! She wished he would stop talking. She wanted his throbbing cock inside her. She didn't want to hear that'd he'd missed her. Didn't want to remember that she'd missed him too while she'd been setting her plans to betray him.

The finger sliding up and down her clit increased in pressure and speed. Virgin could feel her muscles begin to tighten. Could feel the incredibly beautiful sensations swell inside the pit of her womb.

"You like it when I touch you, don't you?" he whispered against her ear.

"You have to ask?"

"I was just wondering since you said I wasn't bad in the sex department."

"Oh for goddess sake!" Virgin gasped. "You do an excellent servicing job."

"Servicing job?" Amusement etched his voice, but she had no more patience for his insecurities.

Locking her legs together she trapped his fingers between her thighs and rode his hand, her hips frantically swiveling as she created much-needed friction. Her brain short-circuited with a sudden burst of pleasure.

"I've never felt this…sexually attracted to a woman in my entire life," he continued slowly as if quite unaware she was climaxing.

"I know it could be the passion poison clouding my mind but I'd like to think there's more going on between us than just sex…"

Sweet Goddess! Did this male ever shut up?

"Later," she managed to croak and grabbed his strong shoulders. "I want you inside of me, Buck. Now!"

He slid two long fingers deep inside her cunt. She just about came up off the bed at the way he wiggled seductively inside her. His thumb took over the seduction of her clitoris. It slid back and forth over her swollen quivering flesh and the wetness of her arousal was slick against the inside of her thighs.

She shook as waves of contractions ripped her apart. Intense pleasure gripped her and she shuddered against the beautiful shards.

"Buck," she managed to plead, wanting his cock, not his fingers, deep inside of her.

Suddenly his fingers were gone and he was coming over her. His large body was moving between her trembling, wide-spread legs.

He came down on her, his heavy body grinding her hips into the corn mattress, his thick, hot spear plunging quickly into her climaxing vagina.

Virgin cried out at the intense way her fevered cunt muscles grabbed onto his rod. Her arms flew around his hard hips, her hands roughly cupping his rock-hard ass cheeks as she tried to pull him in deeper.

A strangled moan erupted from his mouth as he slid in and out of her wet channel with long, strong delicious strokes that only increased the violent spasms rocking her.

"I think I'm falling in love with you, Virgin," she heard him groan from somewhere far away.

She didn't want to talk. Didn't want to think about anything but the beautiful sensation of being fucked by a passion-infected male. She lifted her legs and dug her heels into his firm ass, bringing him even deeper inside her with his every thrust.

"I've grown fond of you too, Buck," she groaned.

She felt the catch in her throat as the truth of her words spread warmth throughout her entire body.

At her confession, he bucked his hips, mercilessly driving his massive penis harder into her. She couldn't stop the cry of arousal from escaping her lips as the spirals of pleasure splashed over her like a brilliant waterfall, allowing her to forget the horrible betrayal she'd set into motion against Buck Hero.

Chapter Seven

Somehow Virgin knew it was a dream but she couldn't seem to stop it from unfolding or diminish the terror it brought to her whole being.

They were coming for her! She could hear their quick determined footsteps as they hurried toward her cell. Sexual tension hummed inside her at the thought of where they would be taking her.

A key grated in her cell door and Virgin held her breath as the three guards rushed inside and quickly grabbed her by her bare arms.

"It's that time again, Virgin. Time to put another bun in the oven." One of the guards sneered darkly. In retaliation, Virgin spat on the guard's face.

"You bitch!" the guard cried out and backhanded her across the face.

The pain splashing against her cheek was a small price to pay. She needed the guards to think she didn't want to go with them. Needed them to believe she hated what they were about to do to her.

"Best not to fight it, Virgin," another guard whispered in her ear as they dragged her naked body kicking and screaming from her cell.

They yanked her down the long hallway, past the cheers and whistles of the other prisoners locked away in cells. Soon she was being shoved inside the room.

Both dread and arousal zipped along her nerves as they hoisted her like a rag doll onto the bed. Within seconds her wrists were tied to the bed's sidebars, her ass propped up on a padded ramp. Her legs were flung over an iron bar and spread ever so wide, her ankles tied to the bar so she couldn't move away from what was about to happen.

Outwardly she cursed them. Inwardly she hummed with sexual arousal. Truth be known, if anyone discovered she enjoyed the machine so much they would have found other more clinical, more boring ways of trying to impregnate her. At least this way she'd been able to look forward to being sexually aroused and satisfied by the fucking machine in this drab prison.

The guards chuckled evilly as the delicious cones were fitted snugly over her breasts.

She bit her bottom lip to prevent herself from crying out shamelessly as the seductive feathery touch of the finger-like objects inside the cones immediately grabbed a hold of her nipples and began to knead and pinch her flesh. Within a split second, her nipples thickened and hardened becoming agonizingly erect with shameless need.

Next came the perfectly fitted clit cone. The guard worked quickly and efficiently and Virgin sighed with excitement as the cone pulsed to life against her clitoris.

When the massive dildo was inserted too quickly and too harshly, Virgin cried out at being impaled so heartlessly.

"This time we'll get you pregnant, Virgin." One of the guards spat. "We've discovered your secret. Discovered why we can't get you pregnant."

A frisson of fear raced through her. They'd discovered her secret?

Sweet Goddess of Freedom, no!

Despite her terror, her body hummed to life as the massive dildo began to slowly move out of her.

"We know your secret, Virgin," the guard continued to taunt.

She gasped as the massive dildo plunged back inside of her. The finger-like objects inside the breast cones stroked her nipples bringing on the familiar arousal of an oncoming climax.

"We know your secret." The guard's words shifted through her pleasure yet again.

"No, you can't know. No one knows." Virgin clamped down on the pleasure threatening to cascade over her senses.

"Yes, we know, Virgin. And you'll be producing male slaves for the rest of your life."

Perspiration dotted her flushed skin as she tried to fight off the passionate effects of the fucking machine. She had to get out of here. Had to break the seductive hold. If they were telling the truth, if they knew her secret contraceptive, then they must have injected an antidote into the machine. If it roared and shot the sperm deep inside of her, she would be impregnated.

She didn't want babies produced in such a cold sterile atmosphere. Suddenly she didn't want to be sexually aroused by a mere fucking machine anymore.

She wanted Buck. Wanted only his children. Wanted to be with him for eternity.

Against her will, the arousal coursed through her. Shivering against the ecstasy growing between her legs, she cried out as the machine slowly began to roar. It was preparing the sperm! Oh Goddess! Stop the machine!

Suddenly Buck's face loomed before her. Disgust blushed his cheeks an angry red.

"You could have had your freedom but instead you betrayed me. Now you can stay here in prison and rot and pop out male slave after male slave for the women to use and abuse."

Oh Goddess of Freedom, what had she done? Why had she betrayed him?

"I'm sorry, Buck. I didn't have any choice," she screamed.

He shook his head wearily and his face began to dissolve. "You should have trusted me, Virgin. You should have trusted me. You've made your bed, Virgin. Now you lie in it."

"Come back, Buck! I'm sorry. Please come back!" she yelled.

The roaring sound grew louder and louder and Virgin continued to scream.

A sharp sting to her cheek snapped Virgin's eyes wide open.

Buck's face loomed right there in front of her, just like in the nightmare.

Yet no anger creased his face. Only concern.

"It's okay. It's just a dream. Just a dream," he whispered as his warm fingers caressed her burning cheek.

Just a dream?

No! It was a nightmare!

Or a premonition?

Virgin shivered violently.

"Hey, take it easy. Everything is fine," he said as he wrapped his protective arms around her.

No. Nothing was fine. And it never would be. Not if she betrayed him.

Despite her feelings of doom and gloom she snuggled her injured cheek onto his broad muscular chest and tried hard to stop herself from shaking.

"I'm sorry I had to slap you. You were hysterical. I couldn't wake you up. Did I hurt you bad?"

She shook her head. The burning his slap created was quickly diminishing.

His arms tightened slightly. "I find it helps to talk out a nightmare. Maybe I can help put things into perspective for you?"

"It was nothing," she lied.

He remained silent and she lay quietly in his warm embrace listening to his strong heartbeat in her ear and to the steady pounding of raindrops against the roof of the shelter.

It felt oddly peaceful listening to the lullaby sound of his steady breathing. She liked the feel of his warm chest pressed against her cheek. Liked his clean masculine scent and loved the interesting way his hand reached across her waist to intimately clasp her fingers with his.

"I was wondering about something," Buck said quietly.

"Hmm?"

"What are you running from?"

Virgin sighed. She wished he would just hold her and keep silent.

"It's a long story."

"I've got all the time in the world. Tell me. I really am interested."

"Why do you need to know?"

Lightning flashed at the tiny windows and his fingers tightened around hers.

"Because I want to know everything about the woman who saved my life."

"Is that the only reason? Because I saved your life?"

"It might have a little to do with it. But there is this thing called sexual chemistry. Some people just connect violently the instant they see each other. Like we did. And now that the passion poison is beginning to wear off I find that I want to get to know you better."

"What do you want to know?"

"You can start by telling me what you're running from."

She could feel the heat of his body pressing so intimately against her skin. The fucking machines were so cold and sterile. They were nothing compared to this male.

Virgin sighed, suddenly wanting to tell him everything.

Wanted to tell him about the fucking machines she'd been hooked up to in prison. Wished she could tell him why she'd taken him from certain death at the hands of the Yellow Hairs and why she'd fucked him in order to save his life, and she ached to explain why she had to betray him.

But she held herself back. Some things she just couldn't tell him.

Other things she could.

"I'm an escaped fugitive from prison."

"Really? You don't strike me as a criminal. What happened?"

There was concern and acceptance in his voice, almost as if he'd been anticipating her confession. She hadn't expected to be surprised at his interesting reaction.

But how else would he react? After all, he was a male. He wasn't a part of society as she was. He wasn't subject to prison sentences like women were when they did something wrong. If a male did something bad, he was merely killed. He didn't have to suffer for endless years by being sentenced to producing future slaves for the cities, villages and hubs.

"I spent thirteen months of a life sentence in prison. I escaped with the help of some friends."

"A life sentence?" To her surprise his thumb brushed erotically against the side of her mouth and she found herself wanting to taste his finger. "You must have done something really bad to end up in prison. What did you do?"

Again, he seemed to be accepting her explanation too easily.

Virgin shook the disturbing thought away. Of course he was accepting what she told him. He was a male. For some insane reason, over the past twenty-four hours she seemed to have forgotten that fact.

"I was framed. Sort of," she admitted, sighing with pleasure at the tender way he traced her upper lip.

"Sort of framed for what?" he asked softly.

"Technically I was convicted of educating several male sex slaves but I really only educated one." She hesitated for a moment as she remembered the raw emotions of what had happened.

"His name was Jarod. He was my twin."

His thumb stilled on her mouth. "Was?"

"He was killed after the Slave Uprising."

"I'm so sorry. It must have been hard for you. I have brothers and sisters of my own and if anything ever happened to my family…" His trailing words were strong and full of passion.

"These brothers? Are they the ones who are educated like you? The ones who have been running around free?"

"Yes."

"And this word, 'family'? What does it mean?" She vaguely remembered mention of that concept during her schooling—something about a past society. She'd never been too interested in theoretical studies. Always preferred practical hands-on classes. Now she wished she'd paid more attention to her schoolwork.

"Family is a group of people who love each other. With the right mix of loved ones, you can feel so safe and secure that it's almost like a drug. You can depend on them, trust them and get support from them, and in return they get the same from you. Yet it goes much deeper than that. It's something right here." He placed a large hand over her heart.

"You know you belong with them and they belong with you. It's such a strong feeling that you'll fight with your very life to keep that feeling safe. You'll fight to keep your family safe."

Virgin knew exactly what he was saying. Family was the reason she'd rescued this male from certain death. It was the reason why she'd fucked him. The reason she wanted him cured and the reason she would ultimately betray him.

"You would do anything to save your family?" she asked.

"Yes, I would."

Virgin grimaced as conflicting feelings bombarded her.

He said he would do anything to protect those other well-hung talking males. He said they were family. If he had the same protective instincts toward his family as she did…

She could use his family to get him to do what she wanted. In a sense, she could use his family to betray him.

The male interrupted her thoughts. "Tell me more about this Slave Uprising."

"You haven't heard of it? I thought everyone had heard of it."

"I come from very far away," he explained.

A rush of excitement burned through her. "From The Outer Limits?"

"It's complicated to explain and right now I want to hear about you."

"You'll explain later? You'll tell me where you come from? Why you're here?"

"I'd like to do that but not right now. Right now I want to hear about you and the Slave Uprising."

Of course he had to be from The Outer Limits. It was a vast, unexplored region. There was no telling what societies lived there.

A couple of years ago the disintegration machines that guarded the sky around their planet had shot down some sort of foreign probe. Rumors had raced throughout the village hubs that the probe had come from a secret society in The Outer Limits, a society with unique technology.

She'd also heard some women theorize the probe had been from Earth, the closest planet with life. But Virgin didn't believe that last rumor. She'd never believed in life in outer space. And she'd never believed the stories and theories that the Goddess of Freedom, the woman who had freed all women from the dominating abusive males by leading a revolt against them centuries ago, had originally come from outer space or from Earth.

Since the disintegration of the foreign space probe there had been talk about sending an exploration team into The Outer Limits to find out what other life existed there, but as far as she knew no team had been assembled as of yet.

Besides it was against the laws to go there. Special passes were only given to Queens and the High Queens so they could worship the statue of the Goddess of Freedom, erected on the beach of Freedom Sea.

And the Yellow Hairs were allowed to roam there to retrieve passion flowers for their highly secret traditions.

Virgin believed what she'd been taught by the Educators, that the original Goddess had come from The Outer Limits centuries ago. Why else would they erect her statue out there?

At the thought of the Goddess of Freedom, a sliver of guilt impaled her. The Goddess had worked so hard to liberate the women from the servitude of males.

And Virgin had tried to undo all her work by breaking the law and educating a male herself. Little had she known that educating her very own twin would ultimately secure her life tenure in prison.

"Jarod was the leader of the Uprising," she continued. "The male slaves took over the entire Brothel Town. Jarod was unable to control them after that. Some of the males mutinied against him; they took many free females against their will, impregnating them. It was horrible."

Buck winced at her words. It gave Virgin a good feeling to know the male didn't approve of forcing females to have sex with them. But she'd already seen that side of him as he'd tried to restrain himself against the passion poison and when he'd asked to be tied down so he wouldn't hurt her.

"During the Uprising, Jarod was caught. I was summoned to see him."

Virgin shivered as she remembered seeing Jarod for the first time in ten years. The teenage boy she'd last seen at nineteen was now a well-muscled, six-foot-three giant. Old and new whip scars crisscrossed over his back and chest and other body parts, proving he had been a difficult sex slave. Bound in chains, his eyes were a cold blue and so dark and dangerous, Virgin had actually been afraid of Jarod for the first time since she'd known him.

"He'd been beaten mercilessly," Virgin continued, "his face and body bruised and battered. He could barely keep his eyes open when he confessed in front of the High Queens that I was the one who'd educated some of his companions as well as himself. His words sealed my fate. I was immediately sent to prison." Virgin could still remember the sharp bite of Jarod's betrayal. The pain tearing through her heart as his dreadful words had seeped through his bruised lips. She'd been so stunned she hadn't even defended herself against the accusations. "He had promised me he would never break my trust. He'd promised never to tell anyone he was educated. In return I had promised I would try my best to change the laws when I became a High Queen."

"Apparently you weren't able to change the laws."

Virgin nodded. "I tried. But shortly after putting out my proposals, the Slave Uprising happened and everything I had worked so hard for died with Jarod's words."

"Why would he betray you? Why would he seal his own fate?"

"I don't know. I thought he was on my side. We hadn't seen each other in ten years. We'd purposely not contacted each other in order to keep our secret safe."

Buck sighed. His hot breath whispered across her forehead. "But someone found out. Beat him until he spilled his guts. Those Queens were so resistant to change they eagerly accepted any way to get rid of you. What happened to the rest of the males?"

"They tried to make deals with the authorities. Wanted improved working conditions. The army was called in. Most of the males were killed. Some of the educated ones were wounded but still managed to escape."

"It's always hard to lose a family member."

That word "family" again. When Buck said that word there was a proud tone in his voice. She wished she could have that proud feeling. To know someone of her own blood cared for her.

But she'd no one as she grew up. She'd never known the woman who bore her. Never known the male whose seed had been supplied. She'd known only Jarod. And there had been something magical between them.

"There was an unexplained bond between us," Virgin said suddenly feeling the need to talk about him. "I felt it the very first time I saw him when we were both young. The minute I saw him I felt as if I were looking into a mirror. Except he was male and I was female.

"Aside from different color of hair, we had the same blue eyes, the same shaped nose, chin, and other similarities we just couldn't ignore. I do believe we were never supposed to know about each other. Never supposed to meet. One day our Educator took us to the Brothel Town to show us how males were trained to be sex slaves. My friend Jacey and I got separated for a few minutes. As we passed an open door to one of the rooms, I caught a glimpse of a male in a cage. Our eyes met and a strange feeling swooped over me. Something sparked in his eyes too. I was drawn to him and entered the room. We stared at each other for a long time and then he grinned."

Virgin laughed as she remembered that happy moment.

"He smiled just like me. It encouraged me to approach the cage. He held his hand up against the bars. He wanted to touch me but I was afraid. We'd been taught that males were dangerous. Instinctively I knew Jarod wasn't dangerous, just curious like I was. I was about to place my hand against his when my Educator rushed into the room and hurried us away. Later, Jacey mentioned how much the male and I looked alike and how odd the Educator had acted in ushering us out so quickly.

"For days I couldn't forget the male. Finally my friend told me I should check his birth record. She knew of someone who worked at the prison and would help.

"Jacey's friend got me into the records room where I discovered Jarod and I were born only minutes apart to the same female with sperm from the same male. I was dumbfounded to say the least."

"And that's when you decided you wanted to get to know him."

"It wasn't easy. Male slaves are never allowed to roam free. He lived in a cage in the brothels, taken out only when his services were required. He knew only the life of a sex slave. But I kept an eye out for him. Eventually I learned the routine they had for him. The only times he was left alone was when they chained him out in the yard in order to tan his body. Or when they chained him in the prison garden where he worked the field to keep his muscles strong. It took several months of sneaking over to see him that I finally managed to teach him the alphabet by writing the letters in the dirt.

When he realized what I was trying to teach him, his whole face lit up with a spectacular need to know more. From then on, I knew that what we females were being taught in school about males was a lie. Males aren't stupid brutes. Jarod proved it. And I was going to prove it, and so we decided I would strive to become a member of the High Five and change the rules where males were concerned."

"But someone found out and got him to confess," Buck said.

Virgin swallowed back the thick lump of betrayal that still overwhelmed her whenever she thought about Jarod.

Buck squeezed her hands in comfort and she felt the stirrings of arousal course deep into her belly again.

"I've got something that'll cheer you up. Want me to try one of my secret fantasies on you?"

She nodded eagerly. Oh, how she needed him again. Needed him to make her forget what his fate would be because of her deceit.

Maneuvering himself around on the bed he suddenly lifted her arms up over her head. Grabbing the ropes she'd used on him earlier, he proceeded to tie her wrists.

Chapter Eight

Excitement shot through Virgin's entire body. She'd never been tied down before. Never been at the mercy of a male in such a way.

"You are a beautiful sensuous woman," he whispered.

Her heartbeat suspended wonderfully in her chest at his words.

He touched his lips to the sensitive curve between her shoulder and neck and cupped the undersides of her generous breasts, holding them out towards himself as if they were two sacred offerings.

Virgin's breath caught at the appreciation shimmering in his eyes. No male had ever looked at her quite this way before and it gave her a warm fuzzy kind of feeling she really liked.

His large thumbs circled her burgundy areolas. Slowly, seductively, he massaged until she responded, her dusky nipples hardening into two aching beads.

"While I was under the passion poison I wanted to do so many things with your body, so many naughty things...and now I've got you as my prisoner."

Her anticipation mounted. "Is that your fantasy? Having your own prisoner to do with what you want?"

He kissed the tip of one throbbing nipple. Her entire breast tingled.

"My own love slave isn't what I'm looking for, Virgin. I want a woman who isn't afraid of experimenting with sex. A woman who wants to try anything I suggest and a woman who isn't afraid of suggesting her own ideas to me."

I'm your woman! she wanted to scream. *I want to experiment with you!*

Sexual hunger, raw and fierce flushed over her like a hot wave.

He drew away from her and leaned over. She heard something being moved across the floor beneath the bed and knew he'd found her secret stash. Items her friend Jacey had given her after she'd helped her escape from prison. Items that every Queen and High Queen owned and didn't go without for very long.

Her heart crashed against her chest as he placed an object wrapped in a towel onto her bare stomach. Something deep inside of her womb sizzled like an inferno as he unwrapped the item and produced the familiar large dildo. A dildo she hadn't had a chance to use yet. A dildo that now looked quite small compared to Buck's massive cock.

His eyes glazed over as he dug something else out from the wooden box. Unwrapping yet another towel, he produced two small nipple clamps, and a one-inch wide velvet belt.

Her excitement soared. "You're full of surprises, aren't you?"

"Surprises I'm sure you'll enjoy."

He removed the items from her stomach and placed them on the narrow cot beside them.

"I've allowed your arm restraints just enough give so that you can sit up."

Her heart fell with disappointment.

"Sit up? Why?"

"Humor me."

Sweet Goddess of Freedom! What was the male up to?

Suddenly every nerve and fiber burst alive with excitement as he slid his hand beneath her back, the warmth of his touch making heated blood hammer through her veins.

In a moment he had her sitting up in a surprisingly comfortable position. Her bare back was pressed against the cool stone wall and her breasts were hanging heavy and free.

She watched wide-eyed as he lifted the velvety belt and looped it behind her neck.

His eyes flashed with dangerous arousal as he took one end of the belt and wrapped it snugly around the base of her breast and knotted it. Leaving the running end of the velvety belt dangling, he took the other end of the belt and did the same to her other breast. He brought the running ends up and behind her neck, tying the two together, which effectively lifted and separated her breasts.

The way he'd bound her flesh made her breasts heat and swell and stick out at him in a pleasing way. Virgin found herself inhaling sharply at the erotic feel of him plumping her nipples by rolling them between his hot firm fingers. Then he lowered his mouth. His warm lips clamped around her sensitive nipple making hot flashes of pleasure zip straight down to her vagina.

He sucked hard. Real hard.

Virgin's back arched, pressing her swollen breast further into his hot mouth. A quick, sharp jab of pain from his teeth, and liquid accumulated between her legs bringing a rush of pleasure flooding her.

She couldn't stop her hips from thrusting upwards.

"Buck!" she gasped.

His mouth left her nipple with a pop and he chuckled.

Quickly he clamped her fiery nipple and began his wondrous mouth magic on her other breast.

His lips burned as he suckled her. The area between her thighs pulsed warmly. Juices escaped her cunt and worked their way down over her lower hole. Her breathing grew heavy and quick. Desperation to have him plunging into her zipped along her nerves, driving her crazy.

His mouth drifted from her swollen breast and he clamped her.

The nipple clamps squeezed her flesh creating a needle-sharp pleasure that radiated through her puffed-up breasts and heated her entire body.

Suddenly his hands wrapped around her ankles. Pulling gently, he eased her down until she once again lay on her back. This time her arms were stretched way over her head and her ass was close to the bottom edge of the bed. Her legs dangled over the edge.

Her bound breasts poked straight up in the air and her nipples were red from his sexy mouth and the nipple clamps. The pressure of having been bound and clamped made her breasts hover at a sweet semi-pain she found quite pleasing.

"You have beautiful breasts," he complimented. "Breasts that will be looked after by these clamps and belt while I tend to other parts down south."

Grabbing a pillow, he got up. She shivered with anticipation at seeing his engorged cock sticking straight out from his body as he strolled to the bottom of the bed. Automatically she lifted and spread her legs giving him full access to her. Through heavy lidded eyes she watched as he crouched.

Her heart crashed against her chest as his lusty gaze fixated between her legs. His head lowered there.

"You've got such a sweet looking asshole, Virgin. Looks like a puckered rosebud," he said without looking up.

She sucked in a breath as he lifted her ass. A pillow was stuffed beneath her buttocks, raising her a few inches off the bed.

"I'm going to make love to you like you've never been made love to before," he whispered. Wild desire ravished his eyes and she couldn't help but moan at the touching sight.

His hands seared against her inner thighs as he kneaded her soft flesh. Slowly he moved higher until he reached her crotch. A thumb slid across her sensitive clitoris and he began a seductive massage.

Virgin closed her eyes and whimpered as her pleasure mounted. He slipped a couple of fingers inside her wet channel. Slurping sounds of her vaginal juices rent the air as his thick fingers slid in and out with sensuous plunges.

When she felt the familiar quivering of her vaginal muscles contracting, Buck slipped his fingers out and lowered them to the crack in her ass.

Her eyes snapped open in surprise as the tip of one juice-streaked finger pushed against her hole. Her virgin anal muscles squeezed warmly around him.

Never in her wildest fantasies had she envisioned that anyone, let alone a male, would probe that part of her anatomy. To her surprise his finger felt really enjoyable as he slid inside. But when he moved deeper, a bittersweet pain bloomed.

Sensing her discomfort he pulled out and then slid back in again. This time the pain quickly faded as he gently worked her hole.

Her belly clenched with the heavenly sensations making her gasp sharply.

"Told you that you'd like it," Buck chuckled. "Want more?"

Virgin nodded, eager to explore this interesting new pleasure further.

He shoved his finger deeper, farther than he'd gone before and tenderly moved around and around.

Her belly clenched tighter as her anal muscles swallowed his finger.

Pleasure played with her senses. She'd never felt this way before. Never imagined something like this could exist.

After he played with her ass for a while, her tense anal muscles gave and relaxed. A second well-lubricated finger joined the other.

Soon he had three fingers inside her and was slowly thrusting in and out.

Before she knew what was happening, a well-lubricated dildo replaced his fingers. The pressure was almost unbearable as he slid it into her ass.

One inch.

Two inches.

Caught off guard by the overwhelming fullness, she began to perspire. A ripple of fear shot through her and she could feel her muscles tighten trying to prevent entry.

"Relax, Virgin. Trust me, you'll enjoy this," Buck whispered.

She did as he asked, telling herself to relax.

It worked. Her muscles relaxed and the dildo slid deeper inside. The pressure turned painful and quickly developed into an erotic pleasure-pain that had her gasping for more.

The pleasure-pain subsided as he withdrew slowly. He lubricated the dildo with more of her cunt juices he'd accumulated and then re-entered.

One inch.

Two inches.

Three inches.

Her thighs automatically widened, demanding more. Her ass clenched around the invasion, the feeling of his penetration flooding her with more breathtaking pleasure-pain.

He withdrew again and soon he was pumping her ass with the dildo.

To her surprise she discovered an arousing tempo. With every outward stroke she tightened her ass muscles and then relaxed them so the lubricated dildo would re-enter her without a problem, sinking deeper every time.

The rhythm stirred those heavenly sensations again and the instant Buck's fingers rubbed against her clit, Virgin's body exploded, making her cry out in shameless bliss.

Without warning, he eased his cock into her spasming pussy.

Her muscles clenched around every bulging vein of his thick shaft.

The pressure of his solid hot flesh and the dildo as he double-penetrated her swooped over her in a tangle of beautiful sensations. Her vagina quivered violently.

"Deeper! Harder!" she commanded.

Buck groaned as he pushed harder with every mad thrust. The pressure mounted in the pit of her womb as her vagina stretched to accommodate his thick, long invasion. White-hot arousal coursed through her veins as his shaft slammed up against her cervix.

"Oh Goddess!" she screamed as the raw sensations overwhelmed her.

Her mind blanked and her hips bucked against him.

Buck began a quick thrust with both the dildo and his heated cock.

Waves of enjoyment built quickly to a crescendo that threatened her sanity.

Her tied hands clenched. Her clamped nipples throbbed painfully. Her bound breasts pulsated.

Her cunt shuddered fiercely as Buck's hot cock and the lubricated dildo pumped in and out of her in a perfectly sensual rhythm.

Furious spasms shredded her and she shuddered beneath the onslaught.

One after another, the mind-blowing seizures hit her. Tormenting her with a violent bliss so beautiful, she screamed.

She quaked from the ecstasy for so long she thought she would die.

Her eyes fluttered open to find Buck furiously thrusting between her widespread legs. His eyes were closed tightly, his breathing intense, raspy.

His cock swelled as he drove into her tight pussy. Leaving the dildo impaled in her trembling ass he now concentrated on his own need for pleasure. Strong masculine fingers dug into the flesh of her hips where he'd grabbed her and held her steady.

Lust-heavy balls slapped against her flesh as he frantically fucked her. The scent of her sexual arousal permeated the air as he continued to drive his hot cock in and out. His entire body stiffened. Throwing his head back he gave a strangled shout and released his heated lust deep into her core.

* * * * *

"The storm is over."

At first Virgin thought Buck's soft whisper was just part of another nightmare trying to get started in her head.

So she didn't move.

Didn't dare break the fullness of the bonds still wrapped around her breasts or shatter the bittersweet pain claiming her clamped nipples. His hot cock was still buried inside her as he lay on top of her, his warm head nestled in the crook between her neck and shoulder.

The seductive memories of being double penetrated rushed to her mind. She almost gasped out loud as she remembered being impaled by both his engorged cock and a dildo. They'd brought such an unbelievable gratification to her.

Pushing a stray hair off her cheek, Buck broke her from her pleasurable thoughts.

Reluctantly she opened her eyes. The steady sound of rain had vanished and the once gloomy interior of the shelter was now bathed in a warm sunny glow.

Virgin swallowed as the harsh reality swamped her senses. Now she had no choice but to put the final phase of her plan into action. A sharp bite of tears crept into her eyes. Truth be told, she didn't want to part with Buck. Deep in her heart she wished they could stay here snuggled in each other's arms for eternity.

But it wasn't possible.

She was a woman.

He was merely a male.

And males and women just weren't supposed to be together or have any kind of affection for one another.

A stray tear slipped out from each of her eyes and blazed a fiery line down her cheeks.

"Why are you crying?"

His soft voice almost unraveled her, yet she forced herself to smile.

"Nothing's wrong."

"Your tears say otherwise." He brushed a hot finger along one tear trail.

She watched dumbfounded as he licked the wetness off the tip of his finger. It was a slow lick of his tongue. A seductive lick, as if her tear was an extraordinary delicacy.

She'd never seen a male slave do this before, to be so bold as to actually taste a woman's tears.

He was an amazing specimen.

"I just wanted this day to last forever," she found herself whispering.

"We can have many days like this, just not here. I want you to come with me. We can have more time to get to know one another."

"I'd like that," she said truthfully. "But..."

"No buts, okay?"

"There's something I have to tell you."

He tweaked a red nipple making her gasp. Instinctively she arched her back pressing her bound breast into the large palm of his hand.

He kissed her earlobe and massaged her breast with agonizingly slow circles.

It felt so wonderful. And yet she had to stop her tumble into the heavenly bliss.

The storm was over and she needed to put the final phase of her plan into motion.

Her gut clenched into an anxious knot.

They would be waiting for him.

"I heard something when I was out walking earlier," she said slowly.

"What's wrong?" A frown marred his face and Virgin hesitated.

Oh how she wished it didn't have to end this way. Once she said it, there would be no turning back and yet it had to be done.

"Your two brothers. They've been captured. They've been taken to the prison."

Chapter Nine

Virgin's heart just about leapt out of her chest as she led Buck through the forest. Now that the final phase of her plan was playing out, indecision and doubt plagued her every step.

Had she done the right thing lying to him about his brothers being captured? Had she done the right thing in trusting the new Queen? Would Cath give Virgin what she'd asked for like she'd said? Or would she betray her as Virgin had just done to Buck?

Up ahead bright lights loomed in the late afternoon sunshine and Virgin's head swam with anxiety.

"I see lights up ahead. Is that the prison?" His harsh whisper broke through her distress.

"That's it, that's the prison," she managed to croak.

"Okay, you stay here. I don't want you harmed. I'm going in for a closer look."

Tears broke from her eyes and the sobs clutched wickedly at her heart as she watched him go.

Toward the prison.

Toward danger.

They would be waiting for him there.

If everything went smoothly she would have what she'd asked for. And yet she couldn't throw Buck away so easily. She knew that now. Knew it without a doubt.

Her heart raced frantically and her mind begged her to do something to stop him from leaving her life for good.

"Wait!" she cried out as she ran after him.

He halted only steps from the tree line. "What's wrong?"

"Don't go. I lied. Your brothers aren't there," she blurted out.

Hot tears streamed down her face. There was no hope left. He would never help her when he learned the truth. But she couldn't let him walk into the trap she'd laid for him.

"I know," he said as he lifted a hand to tenderly wipe away her tears.

"You know?"

She didn't understand. She'd never told a soul about her plan. Not until she'd discussed it with the prison warden.

"I know everything. About the fucking machines impregnating you with your baby son. About how you want to trade him for me. I know all about Cath and her plans to lobotomize all the male babies, including yours."

Virgin blinked in shock.

She saw the pain of betrayal in his eyes and she knew. She knew that somehow he'd discovered why she had taken him from the Yellow Hairs and why she'd saved his life.

Agony paralyzed her. Oh Goddess! He knew!

A sudden rustling in the nearby bushes made her hand sift over the hilt of her knife.

Someone was coming!

Instantly she recognized the tall brown-haired woman clad in shorts and halter-top emerge from the surrounding bushes.

It was her friend, Jacey.

"We followed you from the shelter to the prison, Virgin. We heard everything."

Her old friend grinned and held out her arms. In a split second, Virgin was being held in the woman's warm embrace.

Cradled in her friend's arms, she allowed her racking sobs to break free.

Buck knew. He knew she was going to betray him. He knew she was going to trade him to get her baby back before they destroyed his little mind.

Now it made sense. The odd noises she'd heard when she'd left Buck tied up in the cottage. The strange prickling of warning at the back of her neck when she'd returned from the prison meeting. She'd noticed something amiss but hadn't been able to figure it out.

When she'd left him, Buck had been totally naked. When she'd returned a sheet had been placed over his sex. Before she'd left she'd made sure his restraints had been secure. She hadn't wanted him to escape. When she'd come back she'd noticed the bonds were too loose.

And now that she thought about it, most of the watermelon had disappeared.

Oh Goddess! Why hadn't she seen the signs? They'd been so clear. Had she been so infatuated with him that she'd ignored her very instincts and put herself into danger?

Obviously someone had freed him when she'd been gone. That someone must had been Jacey.

But what if it had turned out to be someone else? Someone who had wanted to throw her back into prison?

Sweet sunshine! The male had been hazardous to her senses and she hadn't even realized it.

It had been a close call. Too close for comfort.

Suddenly another brown-haired woman emerged from the security of the dense trees. Virgin immediately recognized Annie. Until recently she'd been the Slave Doctor of Jacey's village hub. Then she'd run away with one of the talking males.

Another figure joined Annie and Jacey.

A male.

She instantly recognized him as one of Buck's family. They possessed the same height, build and facial features. She'd seen him with Jacey shortly after she and the male had escaped The Breeders hub. On several occasions she'd spied on them having sex. They'd truly enjoyed the pleasure they'd given each other.

Now she knew why Jacey and Annie had run away with their males.

They'd made the women feel special. Made them feel protected. Safe.

Just like Buck made Virgin feel.

Suddenly she realized she, too, wanted to run away with Buck.

But she couldn't. Not until she had her baby safely in her arms. But would he help her after she'd deceived him?

Virgin's blood froze as yet another figure emerged from the surrounding bushes.

It was *the* talking male. The brother called Joe. He'd been strapped to the prison bed a few days earlier; hooked up to the same fucking machine the guards had attached her to in order to impregnate her with his seed.

He was gazing at her now with the same cold, unsmiling green eyes as he'd done in the prison.

And it made her shiver with dread.

The males must have come for revenge. Buck had told her that family always stuck together. Would they kill to keep each other safe?

Quickly she withdrew from Jacey's embrace and took a step back.

"Easy, Virgin. They're here to help," Buck said.

He came up behind her and cradled his large hands snugly around her waist. "We're all here to help you get your son back."

"It's the least we can do since you saved our brother's life."

Buck nodded to the male who'd just spoken. "This is my brother Ben and the big lug over there beside Annie is my brother Joe."

Both males nodded sternly at her. There was no hint of friendliness.

Yet Buck had said they were going to help her get her baby.

She couldn't stop the confusion wrapping around her. Couldn't stop the fresh tears from streaming down her face.

"Don't cry, Virgin. You have to be strong," Buck said as he took her into his arms. "We're going to go ahead with your plan."

"You can't. They'll take you. I'll never see you again."

"It won't go that far," Buck reassured her.

He swung his attention to the others. "What's the status?"

"The area on this side of the meadow is secure," Ben said. "But there's no telling how many guards are staked out on other side of the meadow."

"My section is clear," Jacey replied.

"I saw recent footprints at my post," Annie commented.

"My section was clear," Joe said. "But I just saw Cath at the entrance and she has a baby with her. Time to get into our positions."

* * * * *

"I hope this works," Virgin said tightly from behind Buck as he stepped out into the prison clearing with his hands straight up in the air wearing nothing but his birthday suit.

"I hope so too," he whispered as she prodded him none too gently with the sharp end of the arrow attached to her bow.

He'd figured coming out naked as a jaybird would grab the warden's undivided attention. Now he wasn't so sure he'd done the right thing.

Without clothing he felt vulnerable. Ill at ease. Especially with his brothers' girlfriends getting an eyeful as they watched from their various positions of cover.

Maybe he should have at least worn the pair of shorts his brothers had produced for him only moments earlier.

Maybe he could have concealed a weapon against the small of his back. Just in case.

But that scenario would have been too risky.

Males weren't allowed to wear clothing on this planet.

If he'd given in to his insecurity, the warden would have been alerted immediately. This way he could hopefully distract her with the size of his cock.

"I have what you want!"

At Virgin's shout the warden's head snapped up.

She grinned. It was a cold smile. A smile that sent shivers of doubt racing up his spine.

He hoped they were doing the right thing coming out here in the open like this. Hoped that Joe, Ben, Jacey and Annie were going to be enough of a cover when the time came to make a run for it.

"I see you kept your word. I'm impressed," Cath cooed as she rocked the baby in her arms.

Unmistakable lust shone in her eyes as her gaze zeroed straight onto his cock.

"I want to see the child before I hand over the male," Virgin said. "Step away from the doorway and come closer. We can make the exchange over here in the open."

"You don't trust me, Virgin?"

"I trust you like I'd trust a hungry panther, Cath."

Cath lifted an offended eyebrow. "Even after I gave you my word?"

"Uncover the baby."

"I assure you he hasn't been lobotomized. Although he would have been by the end of today had you not shown up."

"Hold him up!" Virgin snapped.

"Ah, you want to see his birthmark."

The warden stepped closer.

"That's close enough." Virgin warned.

While the warden unwrapped the child, Buck quickly scanned the surroundings.

Nothing moved. And yet he could sense the danger.

Could smell it hanging in the air.

Maybe it was his imagination, but he swore there were others besides his brothers and their girlfriends watching them.

"I assure you he is yours, Virgin," the warden said as she held the naked babe up for Virgin to inspect. There was no sign of the feared lobotomy as the golden-haired child kicked his legs happily and blew a bubble of spit at them.

As Virgin examined the child, Cath studied Buck's cock. Lust and appreciation played havoc in the woman's gaze making him want to cover himself.

He did no such thing.

Let the broad ogle as much as she wanted. It would keep her distracted at what would come next.

He waited for Virgin's signal.

It came quickly.

She coughed twice, the signal the baby was hers and to go ahead with the plan.

He sprang into action.

Moving swiftly, he ripped the babe from the surprised warden's arms. Cradling the warm bundle against his chest, he ran like the devil himself was on his heels.

Behind him, Virgin's arrow whizzed through the air as she cut it loose. It was immediately followed by a screech.

Obviously the arrow had met its mark.

Gunfire screamed all around him and he literally heard the bullets whiz past his head.

Behind him Virgin's anxious breath zipped through the air as she followed him.

The instant he entered the bushes he slowed.

"Keep going!" Virgin screamed. "I'll cover you!"

His gut twisted in turmoil. He should stay and fight. He should give her the baby and let her run.

He did neither. It would take too much time to make the exchange.

Besides, she'd already halted and was firing off another arrow.

Buck did as she commanded and kept running.

* * * * *

The gunfire had ceased a couple of hours ago and Buck anxiously cuddled the cooing baby in his arms at the secluded spot his brothers had indicated as a meeting place.

Thank God, they'd thought about leaving a supply of milk for the kid because he sure was a hungry tyke. As he popped a bottle nipple into the kid's mouth the baby's rosebud lips moved wildly up and down as he suckled.

Buck couldn't help but smile with affection.

He sure was a cute kid. He had the same stubborn tilt to his chin like his mother, the same shiny blonde hair and the same piercing eyes.

It had been well worth the effort to break the kid out of prison.

Cripes! He still couldn't believe what his brothers had told him when they'd found him trussed up like a turkey in the storybook cottage.

That this section of the planet they'd labeled Paradise, which was ruled exclusively by women, used their prisoners and fucking machines to produce future generations.

Kids were raised in the prison system by Nurturers. When the kids reached a certain age they were segregated. Women named The Educators schooled girls, and the boys were trained exclusively to be slaves to the women.

And just recently there had been rumors that all male babies would be lobotomized making them easier to control when they became older and stronger.

Unbelievable.

Sometimes he'd wondered what would happen if the women ruled on Earth instead of men. Now he had an idea and he sure didn't like it.

A twig snapped in the eerie twilight.

His guts scrunched in fear and he was halfway off the log before he spotted Jacey and Annie jogging up the hillside. Sweat bathed their partially clothed bodies, their chests heaved with strained breaths.

The tense looks on their pale faces made uneasiness scream up his spine. Instantly he knew something terrible had happened.

"Where's Virgin?"

The two women exchanged an odd glance that made Buck want to shout his anguish.

"She was captured." Jacey's soft words slammed into his gut and he almost doubled over from the force.

"Where are my brothers?" The anxiety mounted at the thought they, too, might have been captured.

"They'll be here in a minute."

"How the hell did they let her get caught? They promised me they'd protect her!"

"There's more," Annie broke in. "She was wounded."

Sweet Jesus. "How bad?"

"Bad enough," Annie said as she reached out and took the baby from his suddenly shaking arms.

"I'm going back for her," he said.

Before he could take a step, his brother Joe's stern voice shot through the air. "You're doing no such thing, little brother," he said as he and Ben raced into camp.

"Why the fuck not?" Buck hissed.

"Because we've run out of ammunition, that's why. We're going to have to go back to the spaceship and get some more."

* * * * *

White-hot pain ripped through Virgin's wounded side as she inhaled a deep breath.

What in the name of Goddess of Freedom had happened to her? One minute she'd been running from the gunfight, her heart swelling with joy at the thought of her baby safely tucked away in Buck's strong arms, and the next instant something hard and painful had slammed into her right side knocking her clear off her feet.

She'd hit the ground hard, her breath blown out of her lungs. Then she'd promptly passed out only to wake up...

Where was she?

She forced her eyes open.

Familiar gray stone walls greeted her and her stomach sunk like a rock.

Prison.

She'd been recaptured.

Sweet Goddess! Had Buck and her baby also been caught?

Terror at that thought made her cry out.

At the sound of her voice, someone moved in the shadows. She could hear the person breathing. Could barely make out the silhouette of a tall male.

Goosebumps crawled up her bare arms. Instead of hooking her up to the fucking machine this time, perhaps they'd sent a sex slave to impregnate her? She doubted she could fight him off. Not with the pain searing through her side and feeling so weak.

"Virgin? You awake?"

She blinked in shock at the familiar male voice.

Heavy chains clattered in the damp cell as a nude male stepped out of the shadows.

Virgin clamped her hand over her mouth to keep from screaming.

She knew him. He was a one-eyed stranger, yet his face also seemed familiar. Too familiar.

In the glow of light that swept through a narrow barred window in the door, she noted the familiar long black hair that shimmered over his shoulders and cascaded like a midnight waterfall all the way to his brown nipples.

"You're alive?" she whispered.

The chains clattered again as he crouched down beside the prison bed on which they'd placed her.

A smile touched the corners of his full lips. "It is me, Jarod, your twin."

A wide eye the dark blue color of Freedom Sea stared down at her. A black patch covered his left eye. A jagged scar reached out from under the patch and streaked down the left side of his cheek ending beneath his earlobe.

Suddenly she felt as if she were in some sort of dream. Her dead twin was alive. How could this be possible?

She lifted her hand and touched the raised scar. "What did they do to you?"

For one brief instant an icy look flooded her brother's face making Virgin shiver, but the frigid look quickly melted replaced instantly by concern.

"It is the question I should be asking of you. How do you feel? I cleansed the gunshot wound as best I could with the items they gave me. But I'm no doctor."

"Jarod, you did a good job. I'm fine," she lied.

The pain in her side seared like a hot poker brand but it was nothing compared to the pain clenching her heart at the thought of her twin losing an eye and what he must have endured over the past year.

"They promised to bring a Quick Healing Injection for you, but that was hours ago," he said.

Virgin let her fingers trail over the deep blue bruises shadowing her twin's strong jawline.

"They told me you were dead." She let her hand drop as emotions she couldn't put a name to suddenly welled up inside her.

"They told me you had escaped," he said.

"I did. But I came back for the baby. Buck and some others helped me. I don't know if they got away," she babbled as the tears burst free.

His warm hand curled over her shoulder in a gentle squeeze.

"The guard spoke of you being the only one captured."

"Thank the Goddess of Freedom." That's all that mattered right now. Her baby and Buck were safe.

"I had heard they'd impregnated you." Jarod's voice sounded angry. Strained. "I wanted to help you but they kept me under constant guard in the prison and at the Brothel Town."

Virgin shivered at his words. Brothel Town. It meant only one thing. They'd returned him to being a sex slave.

"I'm surprised they didn't cut out your tongue or worse because you're educated."

"A tongue is too useful for what is required of me."

She found herself blushing at his words and at the memories of Buck's tongue probing deep inside her only hours ago.

She wondered what Buck must think of her. Wondered how angry he must be at her for attempting to betray him. It didn't count that she'd warned him at the last minute. Didn't matter that he'd known all along she'd wanted to use him to trade for her baby.

What she'd done to him was wrong. Yet he'd still saved her child.

And she'd been captured.

And if she hadn't been caught, she would never have known about her twin being alive.

Jarod's one eye brightened. "So it is true? There are other talking males that helped you? Were they my friends, Taylor and Blackie?"

"I don't know what happened to your friends, Jarod. The last I heard they disappeared into The Outer Limits."

He winced and closed his eye. "That was our original plan before I was betrayed."

"By who?"

Jarod frowned. "Aren't you curious as to why I betrayed you?"

Virgin shrugged. "They beat you. You didn't know what you were saying."

"That's no excuse."

"It wasn't your fault. We were all deceived. Someone wanted me out of the way. Someone didn't want the laws to be changed."

"I think someone is coming."

Suddenly he stood and the chains between his ankles and wrists clanged as he headed to the thick-planked door.

It was then that Virgin heard numerous footsteps click upon the rock floor.

And they were approaching fast.

"Do what you have to do to get out of here, Virgin. Don't think about me, just—"

The sharp sound of the bolt being lifted from the other side of the door cut him off.

Instantly he backed away as the heavy door swung inward. Three guards swooped inside like vultures; two of them grabbed his shackled arms. The third guard quickly placed a penis leash on him.

"Leave him alone!" Virgin cried out.

She struggled to get out of the bed but pain lanced through her side making her fall flat onto her back.

Perspiration dampened her, chilling her to the bone.

She watched helplessly as the guards threw Jarod up against the stone wall. Rage lit up his eye but he didn't do a thing to protect himself.

Why wasn't he struggling? Why didn't he overpower them and rush out the open door?

"I said leave him alone!" she screamed.

"I'm sure you had a nice visit with your twin, Virgin."

Dread filled her as the prison warden, Cath, strolled into the cell. Her right arm hung in a sling, compliments of the arrow Virgin had embedded in her shoulder when she'd reached for her weapon earlier in an attempt to stop Buck from escaping with her baby.

"I assume he tended your wound as instructed," Cath said.

"She needs a Quick Healing injection as I instructed," Jarod growled.

Virgin didn't miss the third guard, the one who'd efficiently placed a penis leash on him, groping his half erect penis with her hands. It disgusted her to watch her twin being fondled by women who had no interest in him except to satisfy their lustful urges. He deserved better than that. He deserved a woman who cared for him.

The way she cared for Buck.

At the thought of Buck, Virgin inhaled a shaky breath. Would she ever see him again? Would she ever see her baby?

"She'll be given a Quick Healing Injection only when she has agreed to my terms," Cath said smoothly.

She reached out and tried to grab Virgin's nipple, but Virgin swatted her hand away, covering herself with the sheet that had slipped off when she'd tried to help him.

"You dare to strike me?" the warden gasped in anger.

"I'll do much worse to you if you touch her again!" Jarod bit out furiously.

Cath whirled on him. For a moment she thought Cath would strike him with the stun baton she carried in her hand, but she didn't.

Instead, she smiled. It was the smile that had made Virgin's blood grow cold many a time during her year in prison.

"And exactly what would you like to do to me, Jarod?" Cath spat.

"Break your neck for starters."

A muscle twitched in the warden's left cheek.

Past experience had taught Virgin the twitch meant she was ready to explode at the slightest provocation. And it wasn't pretty when she did. Cath had injured many guards and prisoners because of her short temper. She hadn't always been like that. The Slave Uprising had changed her.

Rumors had flown she'd been gang-raped by some of the males who'd taken over the Brothel Town last year. Others had said she'd fallen in love with a sex slave who'd spurned her during the revolt.

Whatever had happened to her, Cath had changed into a bitch, a bitter woman who inflicted pain and brutality on a mere whim. And Virgin had been the brunt of it many times. Especially when she'd been pregnant.

"Hmmm, such brutal honesty becomes you, lover," Cath said.

Lover? Virgin's guts crunched into a sickening knot.

"Unfortunately, I prefer my males strong and silent." Cath nodded to the guard who was now playing with Jarod's balls.

The guard reacted quickly. Drawing something out of the bag she carried at her waist, she efficiently trussed a ball and gag into his mouth.

"There that's better. Strong and silent."

In response, Jarod glared back at her. His one eye looked so dark, it reminded Virgin of the day he'd confessed to the High Five Queens that she'd been the one to educate him and his friends.

"Now back to the matter at hand." Cath returned her attention to Virgin. "You will do what I ask."

"Stuff yourself into a boiling pot of water, Cath. I'll do nothing you ask."

"Not even if it insures the continued good health of your twin?"

"He doesn't look like he's been well taken care of so far."

Cath smirked. "I don't know why I never dangled his life over your head while you were in prison. Perhaps because I was amusing myself too much with him to give you much thought, aside from the beatings I gave you when your twin was difficult with me."

She let her words dangle over Virgin's head.

Now it made sense, why Cath had shown up numerous times at her cell and seemed irritated without reason. She'd assumed the woman simply enjoyed tormenting her. But now she'd indicated she'd made Virgin's prison stay a virtual hell to get back at Jarod.

Another thought struck her. Could the rumors be true about Cath falling in love with a sex slave?

Was Jarod the male Cath had fallen in love with?

That thought made Virgin's blood boil with anger.

"You are the coldest, cruelest bitch I've ever come across, Cath Smart!" Virgin hissed.

"Silence! Or I will have your twin whipped and you too!"

Virgin clamped down on a sharp retort.

"Now! I once again have your attention." Cath sat down on the edge of the bed. "In order to keep your twin alive, you will allow me to do with you as I please."

Virgin held her breath as Cath grabbed the sheet from her clasped hands. The urge to slap the horrible woman was so great that Virgin almost did it, but she had to protect Jarod.

Had to do what Cath wanted.

For now.

Thank the Goddess of Freedom, Cath didn't attempt to touch her again. But the lust shining in those evil eyes as the woman's gaze roved greedily over her bared breasts was enough to nauseate Virgin.

"I've always admired your breasts, Virgin. They're plump and perky. Your nipples are unique. They are large and suckable and such an unusual dusky color. And I'm sure your breasts feel just as silky as they look."

"What do you want from me, Cath?"

"I want you, of course. I've always wanted you as my mate. To have you as my own would be a treasure. I've seen the way the other prison women look at you. They admire those large nipples. They lust after your delicious looking pussy lips."

Virgin tensed at Cath's words.

A low growl sifted past the ball gag in Jarod's mouth.

"Quiet, slave!" Cath snapped at Jarod, and then returned her gaze to Virgin's bared breasts.

"What's in it for me?" Virgin asked as she tried to keep her voice from shaking with anger and disgust.

"Lots of pleasure and I'll let you see your twin whenever you wish."

Virgin glanced at Jarod who stared back at her with his icy-cold eye, his head shaking a warning.

"I'll do what you want, if you set Jarod free."

"How noble of you, dear. There is no negotiating. He stays."

"Then I won't do anything you want."

Without warning Cath's hand lashed out and grabbed Virgin by her hair. Pain seared into her head as she was tugged forward until her face was only inches from Cath's.

"You are in no position to bargain, Virgin. Let me put it another way. You will accept my terms or your twin dies."

Virgin bit back a violent curse as Cath let go of her hair and stood.

"Take him back to his cell. Prepare him for me."

Virgin's heart sank as lusty giggles erupted from the guards. The chains holding Jarod hostage clanked through the cell as he was quickly ushered out.

Cath stopped at the doorway. Without turning, she said coldly, "You will do as I say, Virgin, or your twin dies. For real this time."

* * * * *

After they'd taken Jarod away, a guard had come and administered a Quick Healing Injection to Virgin.

The drug worked quickly, easing the pain from the gunshot wound allowing her to stand and frantically pace the cold, damp cell.

Goodness! She couldn't believe Jarod was alive!

But he'd endured so much. Suffered as all male sex slaves suffered. And he would continue to go through hell for the rest of his life.

Unless, she did something to help him.

And she would do something, even if she had to sacrifice herself.

Chapter Ten

"You're a natural father." Ben chuckled as he slapped Buck heavily on the back jolting the sleeping babe Buck rocked snugly in his arms.

Buck swore quietly as the baby's rosebud lips pursed at the rude intrusion. Thankfully the kid didn't wake up.

"Cripes, don't do that! I just got the kid to sleep," he hissed beneath his breath.

"My apologies, papa."

"Don't call me that."

"Why not? You like Virgin. And the kid comes with the great-looking package."

"She's not a package."

"Testy, aren't we?" Ben grinned.

"If you want to carry on a conversation with yourself, go over there where we can't hear you."

"Aye, aye, Papa." Ben saluted and quickly scooted out of the way before Buck's foot could connect solidly to his shin.

Sometimes his brother could be a son of a bitch, Buck thought as a few minutes later he lowered his precious cargo into the makeshift basket he'd made using twigs from nearby trees and lined with a soft blanket.

"Where the hell is Joe with that ammo, anyway?" Buck growled as a moment later he joined Ben on the log in the middle of their camp.

"Hey, take it easy," Ben said. "He practically just left. He won't be back till morning, if that."

"I'm getting sick of sitting around with my fingers stuck up my ass doing nothing when the woman I—" Buck shut up before he said something he shouldn't be saying, let alone be thinking.

"The woman you what?" Ben's eyes flashed with humor in the twilight.

"Shut up."

"You heard Joe before he left. Orders are to sit tight till he gets back with the ammo. And when Jacey and Annie come back they'll tell us exactly where Virgin is. We'll swoop in and grab her."

"That's it? That's all you gotta say?"

"What the hell else do you expect? You want us two to go in defenseless? Besides we have a kid to babysit."

Frustration ripped Buck's guts apart as he thought of the baby. If he kept sitting here doing nothing the kid wouldn't have a mother. He had to do something and he needed to do it now.

He stood and headed out of camp.

"Where are you going?"

"Gotta take a leak," Buck lied. "Watch the kid, will you? I'll be back in a minute."

Buck slipped into the darkness and when he was far enough away from the camp, he broke into a run.

* * * * *

He was not in love with Virgin, he thought as two hours later he was still jogging. Repeat, he was not in love with the gorgeous blonde.

Then why in hell was his heart dying at the mere thought of what might be happening to her? Why was he cursing a blue streak with each and every step that took him through the darkness towards God knew what?

He didn't even know for sure where she was. He was walking blind. Literally. Even the moon had deserted him behind a veil of clouds.

Damn!

He should be calming himself down. Should stop walking toward that prison.

He wasn't even sure that's where they'd taken her.

But where else would they take a fugitive, right?

Buck cursed violently under his breath.

Why in hell had he left her behind? He should have given her the kid and let her go instead of him running off like some coward. He should have been more protective of her.

Truth was his judgment had been clouded. He'd still been silently fuming about her deception.

When Joe, Ben and those two women had found him in that storybook cottage, naked and tied up…

Man! He hadn't been so embarrassed in his life. Well, actually he hadn't been so embarrassed since Virgin had first sucked him off but that was beside the point.

Thankfully, upon his being discovered his brothers had acted quickly in getting him out of those restraints. The woman sure had been amused seeing him naked and tied up. His brothers had been happy to find him too.

They'd come to the secret hideout to ask Virgin if she'd by any chance seen any sign of him and lo and behold had found him happily being held captive.

He'd explained how he'd been infected with passion poison and shortly after that the women had left to catch up with Virgin.

While they'd been gone his brothers had teased him immensely as they'd attacked the watermelon.

What he wouldn't do to have Virgin stuffed safely in that cottage with a fresh batch of cool watermelon for them to play with.

A smile zipped across his lips at that heavenly thought.

The joyful feeling in his guts was short-lived when he spotted the prison lights.

Upon reaching the outskirts of the prison yard, he crouched behind the trees.

The ugly building loomed against the night sky like something out of a gothic novel. It gave him the creeps.

Last time when Virgin had brought him here, he'd known she was deceiving him. Known about the baby.

The women had told him when they'd come back. In the storm, they'd taken a shortcut from the prison to the storybook cottage in order to warn Buck and his brothers about the deal they'd overhead Virgin making with the prison warden.

His guts had crunched violently upon hearing that tidbit.

And he'd finally realized why she'd rescued him. Finally understood why she'd saved his life by fucking him for all those hours.

Upon hearing the news about being betrayed, his first impulse had been to abandon the shelter, leave Virgin and simply forget about her.

Unfortunately he hadn't been able to do that. He'd understood why she'd done it.

He would have done the same thing for any one of his family members in similar circumstances.

Yet it brought him little relief to think she hadn't trusted him enough to tell him about her child and that she would so easily have betrayed him.

And here he was ready to put his life on the line to save her.

Heck, maybe he was in love.

* * * * *

Virgin cringed at the sound of footsteps approaching the cozy room where the guards had put her after she'd sent her affirmative answer to Cath's terms.

Oh Goddess of Freedom! Could she actually go through with this? Could she actually have sex with Cath?

Virgin closed her eyes and lay back on the fluffy bed to wait.

She had to go through with this. There were no other options. It was the only way to get close enough to her in order to get the stun baton Cath always carried.

She'd felt the horrible sting of the stun baton many times while in prison. But Cath had always had plenty of guards around her to prevent her victims from retaliating.

Rumors had it Cath preferred not to have guards around while having sex. Virgin prayed those rumors were true.

The sour knot in her stomach twisted violently as a key grated in the lock.

A moment later the door swung inward and Virgin recoiled inwardly.

Cath stood in the doorway, wearing nothing more than a flimsy see-through veil similar to hers. It left little to her imagination.

Medium sized, drooping breasts and red nipples poked against the material and a dark mass of hair was visible between her legs.

This time Cath wasn't wearing her arm in a sling, proof that she'd taken a Quick Healing Injection.

Virgin blew out a thankful breath when she spotted the stun baton and a disintegration gun in Cath's hand.

"Did you have a bath and shave your cunt as I instructed?" Cath asked as she closed the door and strolled into the room.

Virgin forced a smile and nodded.

"I think I'm going to have quite a bit of fun with you, Virgin." Cath cooed as she headed toward a closet in the far corner. Virgin had already tried to open it in an attempt to find a weapon, but it had been locked.

She knew what was inside. She'd heard the rumors about Cath being a Dom and that she harbored every sex toy imaginable. She also loved to inflict pain on her lovers. Unfortunately Virgin wasn't into pain and she sure wasn't into wanting to have sex with Cath.

But she had to keep Jarod alive. And she would do anything to keep him that way. Just like she would have done anything to keep her baby or Buck safe.

Family always sticks together.

She remembered the proud way Buck had mentioned the word family.

At the thought of him, pain clutched at her heart. She missed him terribly.

Yet if she could somehow get at Cath's stun baton she could break out of here, especially since Cath hadn't tethered her in chains as was mandatory for all prisoners. That error might prove fatal for the prison warden.

The guards had brought her to this fancy room with the big soft bed, fluffy white carpets and barred windows. Virgin hadn't missed the metal cuffs and chains cemented into the far wall, or the breast torture machine and other torture devices littering the room.

She shivered with revulsion when Cath lifted a double-ended dildo from the closet and her stomach dropped in disappointment as Cath hung the stun baton and gun on a hook and closed the door.

Oh sweet Goddess of Freedom! How in the world was she going to get out of here now?

Think, Virgin! Think!

But her mind blanked as Cath drew closer to her with the dildo. It was huge, bigger than Buck's shaft if that were possible. She wondered how many other women had endured what Cath wanted to do to her.

"I can tell you like it. It must remind you of the talking man's cock. I daresay I understand why you would want to keep him all to yourself," Cath said as she gingerly placed the dildo on the pillow and gazed down at Virgin.

"Now, I want you to take off your veil," she said softly.

Virgin cursed inwardly. It wasn't as if Cath hadn't seen her naked before. All women prisoners were required to wear no clothing while incarcerated.

But this time was different. This time she'd agreed to have sex with Cath.

Hesitantly her shaky fingers slipped to the collar of the flimsy garment that she'd discovered laid out on the fluffy bed.

"I want you to take it off slowly. Seductively."

Virgin forced a tight smile and lifted the veil as slowly and seductively as she could under the circumstances.

When the flimsy garment was fully off her, Cath inhaled a satisfied breath.

"I've wanted to fuck you for as long as I can remember, Virgin. But I wanted to wait until after you gave birth. And then you escaped."

She flinched as Cath's hands reached out and her fingers probed the bullet wound in Virgin's side.

"The Healing Injection works wonders, doesn't it? In a couple of days the only thing left will be a pretty little scar."

Virgin closed her eyes as Cath suddenly cupped her breasts. The warden's flesh felt cold and clammy as she tested the weight of her breasts, her thumbs caressing Virgin's plump nipples.

"So soft, so velvety. So beautiful." Cath licked her lips and Virgin swore she would scream if Cath decided to lower her mouth over her nipples.

She wanted to swat those clammy hands away. Wanted to run out of the room screaming. Wanted to stop this insanity.

"Your breasts are exquisite jewels," Cath said as she continued to rub Virgin's nipples.

To her horror, her nipples betrayed her and actually hardened with arousal.

"I can't wait to claim you. To be there when those gorgeous nipples are pierced at our mating ceremony. I've ordered your clit to be pierced too, of course. And I have such heavy weights for those clit rings. You will be required to wear the weights always so you will be aroused and wet for me whenever I require you, which will be quite often. As you've probably already heard, I have a ravenous sexual appetite. And I will adorn you with the newest nipple rings on the market. I've already sent the prison doctor to pick them up. I want everyone to know that you will be my new mate."

Sweet sunshine! She swore she was going to puke.

"And of course you'll be able to see your twin whenever you like as I said. I've sent for him. He should be here shortly to show you how to pleasure me. I will have both of you pleasuring me at the same time. It will be so wonderful!"

Virgin's eyes snapped open in shock.

Jarod was going to be her teacher? Both of them would have to have sex with Cath?

Insanity! Virgin's mind screamed.

Cath's fingers gave Virgin's nipples a cruel twist. It hurt. Not a sexy hurt like Buck's teeth when he'd nipped her during their watermelon sex, but a pain she didn't think she could tolerate for very long. But endure she must.

She tried hard not to lower her gaze to the closet where Cath had left the stun baton. Hopefully there would be time to grab it later when Cath was more involved in the sexual foreplay.

"In order to give you a taste of the pleasure-pain the rings can create, we'll start you off with the nipple clamps. They'll desensitize you for the rings which I've ordered fitted sometime tonight."

Oh great.

Thankfully Cath let go of her breasts and leaned over and sensuously stroked the thick, rubber double-ended rod.

"But first we're going to fuck each other with this gorgeous double-ended dildo that I just purchased especially for us. Do you see the clit pleasures on both ends? Oh, I can't wait!"

Virgin jolted as a harsh knock came swiftly at the door.

"Who is it?" Cath shouted eagerly. Obviously she hoped Jared had arrived.

"There is something that requires your immediate attention," came a guard's excited voice.

"Take care of it!" Cath shouted back with impatience. Her lusty gaze lowered to Virgin's clamped legs.

"Spread your legs wide for me. I want to see you exposed fully."

No! She could do this!

"This is important." The guard's voice was louder this time, more insistent.

Suddenly there was a commotion in the hallway and to Virgin's horror, the door swung inward.

She gasped at the sight of two guards holding an unconscious Buck between them. Blood flowed freely from a bullet wound in his upper right shoulder.

The scream twisting around in Virgin's mind found its way to her throat and out of her mouth.

* * * * *

Virgin's emotions were on a rollercoaster. She felt lightheaded. Her thoughts sped so fast through her head she couldn't make sense of them. One thing did stick however.

Buck had come back for her.

Upon dumping Buck's unconscious body on the pristine white carpet in Cath's fancy room, Cath had quickly ordered the guards to remove Virgin.

Now as her cell door crashed shut behind her, Virgin's thoughts went haywire.

She'd recognized that greedy sparkle in Cath's eyes when she'd seen Buck slumped between the guards. And Cath hadn't hesitated in removing the shorts from Buck's body revealing the impressive shaft that lay limp between his thighs, not to mention the perfect matching set of heavy balls.

Virgin knew as soon as Cath could, she would hook Buck up to the fucking machine, just as she'd done to his brother, Joe. She would use his seed to start impregnating the prisoners. And this time there wasn't a damned thing Virgin could do to stop the women from conceiving.

Chapter Eleven

Buck had the oddest awareness that someone stood nearby. Watching him. He could sense the evil slithering through the air all around him. Could hear the coarse inhalation of her breath. Could smell incense sifting through the air.

Something soft and warm cradled the underneath parts of his body. Instinctively he knew he lay on a carpet.

Cool air slapped against the rest of him. He didn't have to open his eyes to know he was naked.

Again.

These ladies sure liked their men on visual display.

Keeping them men naked. Humiliating them. Embarrassing them.

He winced at the throbbing pain radiating from his shoulder. The pain was bearable. Barely.

His brain felt sluggish though. Slow to respond, probably due to loss of blood. So he lay there and tried to focus on what had happened.

It all came back to him slowly, in bits and pieces.

He finally managed to put it all together and his stomach soured at his stupidity. He'd been shot while trying to gain access to a secluded back door behind the drab looking prison. He must have tripped some silent alarm or something, because he'd heard footsteps approaching.

He'd run. Thought he'd made it safely into the trees without being seen but a bullet had taken him down. And by the ache in both front and back, he knew the bullet had gone clean through him.

Shit!

He'd screwed up. Big time.

He'd gotten himself caught. He was useless to Virgin now. And he'd put his brothers' lives in danger as well because he knew without a doubt they'd come and try to break him out.

He was an idiot coming here without a plan.

Being found naked and trussed up in the storybook cottage by his brothers was nothing compared to this dumb stunt.

He would never live this down. He wouldn't blame his brothers if they never asked him to accompany them on another space mission. Hell, if NASA got wind of how stupidly he'd acted by going after a woman he barely knew, a woman he believed he might be in love with…

Ah man.

The love word. Not good.

If love scrambled a man's brains so bad that he couldn't even think straight, then they could keep it.

The footsteps padded away from him taking with it the sense of evil. He sighed with relief at the sound of a door opening somewhere to his left. Heard water running. Heard a woman humming.

Now was his chance to get the heck out of here.

Gingerly he tried to roll to his right side. White-hot pain slammed through his shoulder, zipping up his neck and slamming straight into his brain, encouraging him to keep still.

Damn, but he was screwed.

He forced his sticky eyes open. At first he saw a blurred room, then slowly it rolled into focus.

It was quite an interesting room. He didn't miss the shackles cemented into the walls and torture devices nearby. It contrasted greatly with the décor.

The sheets on the nearby bed were flowery in soft shades of orange and greens. The walls were white-washed cement. Forest green curtains adorned windows.

Windows with bars.

Lovely touch.

His gaze flew to the red-tinged moon hanging in the sky and he shivered. Blood on the moon. Someone would die tonight.

He sure hoped it wasn't anyone he knew.

A rap at a nearby door made Buck start. He closed his eyes just in time to hear quick-paced footsteps pass by him and along with it came that creepy sense of evil.

As he heard the creak of a door opening, cooler air drifted against his naked body.

He tried not to wince as the irritating clatter of metal shackles entered the room. Through narrowed eyes he noticed a big, muscular black-haired man with a black patch over one eye hobble into the room.

Buck closed his eyes.

"Who is he?" the man's hoarse voice asked.

"He's the one who tried to help Virgin today."

"The talking male?" Curiosity etched the man's voice. "What happened to him? He's bleeding."

"He was shot trying to break in to get Virgin. He's lucky it wasn't a guard with a disintegration gun. He'd be quite dead now."

"He looks pretty close to it right now."

"Not to worry. He's been tended to with a Quick Healing Injection. He'll be up and about soon enough and then I'll be able to check out the merchandise. First however, I want to deal with you."

"So, deal."

Buck could hear the sound of hands sliding upon flesh and he opened one eye to watch.

Cripes.

The woman was all over the guy like a wet tuna fish sandwich. Her hands slid feverishly over his broad chest. A chest heavily banded with impressive muscles and a whole lot of scars.

Ouch.

The guy stood stock-still as the warden grabbed him by the balls and squeezed. Obviously he didn't want to participate in the warden's lust. The heavy shackles clamped around his wrists and ankles weren't encouraging the guy to participate either.

"Was it true what you said earlier in your sister's cell? Would you really break my neck with those large sensual hands that bring me so much pleasure?"

His sister's cell?

"You touch Virgin and I will kill you."

Virgin? His sister?

It took Buck a good few seconds to digest that tidbit of information.

Was this guy, Virgin's twin? Was this Jarod?

But he was supposed to be dead. He opened his other eye to get a better look.

Aside from long black hair, he did have Virgin's facial features. Same stubborn chin. High cheeks. Blue eye.

What was he doing alive? He was supposed to be dead.

"She didn't seem to mind my touch when she agreed to my proposal," the prison warden cooed.

"What did you do to her?" Jarod's question echoed Buck's thoughts.

"Not to worry. She wasn't here against her will."

The woman drew away from the guy and padded over to a nearby table where she picked up a piece of paper.

"This document states that Virgin will be a free woman."

Buck blinked in shock.

The male's one eye narrowed with suspicion.

"Why are you pardoning her?"

"Because she's agreed to be my mate."

Buck's heart picked up speed.

The prison warden's mate? Virgin? Had she flipped?

"I'm having her fitted with the nipple and clit rings shortly. New technology developed has implanted tiny chips in the rings. If Virgin decides to run, she will immediately be disintegrated by the drones."

"She knows of this?"

The prison warden shrugged. "I haven't told her."

Buck sensed the carefully restrained anger in the man.

Could also feel it building in himself. He struggled hard to keep still, fought to keep himself from panicking. He needed to find Virgin now more than ever. Needed to get to her before she was outfitted with those deadly nipple rings.

"You'd better tell her. Or your new mate may be dead within minutes of receiving it and you won't be getting any more pleasure from me," the guy with the patch said.

"You think she'd go against her word? She's agreed to be my mate. Allowed me to touch her as proof of it. It would be a pity if she were disintegrated, wouldn't it?"

"Wouldn't look good for your image, Cath."

"That's true. It might make any future mates wary of me, and I wouldn't want that. Now what would you do for me in return for my telling Virgin about her disintegration rings?"

Blackmail. Clever bitch.

One of the man's heavily muscled arms lifted and he gently caressed the curve of one of her thinly veiled breasts.

The prison warden purred.

Buck's stomach soured at the sound.

"I want you to fuck me, Jarod," she whispered.

The clatter of chains split through the air making Buck close his eyes. A breeze of air feathered over his body as the two walked past him.

Squinting his eyes open again, Buck watched the prison warden lead the naked man to the far wall.

Once there he allowed her to place a heavy metal collar around his neck.

"Close collar," she whispered.

To Buck's surprise the collar closed on its own.

Apparently the collar was voice activated. Interesting. The women on this planet were more civilized than he'd anticipated.

He noted the half-inch thick chain that dangled from a hook in the collar. The other end was secured to a bolt in the wall. The chain stretched a few feet allowing the man to sit on the bed where he held out muscular arms so the warden could unshackle his wrists. She did the same with his ankle shackles.

When he was free, except for the collar and chain that would prevent him from leaving the room, the warden stared down at him.

Buck could see the way her breasts heaved beneath her veiled clothing as she inhaled with anticipation. Slowly she lifted her arms.

The man stood. Grabbing the hem of her dress, he slowly lifted it up baring her abdomen, belly, breasts and then he tugged it off.

"Suck my tits," she instructed. "Suck them hard. I want you to bite them. Make me hurt. Make me hurt bad."

From the angle where he lay, Buck couldn't see the man's face, but by the tense way he held his shoulders, he bet the guy wasn't really into what the warden wanted.

But he did what the warden instructed.

His head lowered and latched onto one of her budded nipples.

Her eyes widened in pain and then she gasped as Virgin's brother began to do his job. His head bobbed sideways and up and down. Suckling sounds intermingled with her whimpers.

Soon she was a writhing mass.

The man pushed her backwards and she disappeared from Buck's view as she fell onto the bed.

Buck felt his eyes widen at the huge erection on Jarod. His heavily veined cock pulsed purple and the swollen head was mushroom shaped.

The guy was well-hung, just as big as his brothers and himself.

No wonder he'd been procured as a sex slave.

Suddenly the man's head swung around and he made eye contact with Buck.

Shit!

No use closing his eyes; Jarod had seen him watching.

A bolt of fear cleaved into his spine as he waited for him to tell the warden her captive was awake.

He said nothing. Instead, he simply shook his head slowly and whispered the word no.

And then he lowered himself over the woman and disappeared from view.

Buck didn't know how long he lay there listening to the guttural moans of Jarod and the hisses and whimpers from the warden, but it seemed like a lifetime.

He could only hope that Virgin wasn't being outfitted with the deadly nipple rings yet. And he hoped like heck he'd understood correctly that Jarod's shaking of his head and the no on his lips meant for Buck to stay put.

But the longer the fucking went on, the more frustrated and anxious Buck became.

Soon the warden's sensual moans died away and silence split the air.

Buck tensed as the one-eyed man emerged out of the darkness.

He hunched down beside Buck and grinned. "She always passes out when I fuck her."

Oh man, too much information.

"Here, take this."

Buck's eyes widened as the sex slave thrust an odd-looking gun in front of his face. Was this guy serious? Or was he setting him up?

"Why don't you use the gun yourself?" he asked cautiously.

"Can't." Jarod said and touched the metal collar around his neck.

Buck had forgotten it was voice activated.

"Why don't you use the gun on her? Make her say the right words."

The guy's grin widened.

"Obviously there are many things about this prison you don't know, talking man. There are sensors everywhere on the inside. Every day she enters a new password into the system. All she has to do is say the secret word and the guards will be here. Even if she's gagged, her words will be understood. Come, let me help you up."

To Buck's surprise, the pain in his shoulder had lessened to some degree but not enough to prevent him from getting light-headed as the big guy hustled him to his feet.

"Virgin is in cell number thirteen in Cell Block C. Follow the signs. Once you get to the entrance go into the Security room. The room will be empty now. The guard is on her rounds for the next hour. All you have to do is flip the switch with the number 13. Do you understand?"

Buck nodded as the sex slave handed the gun to Buck. Once again he got the feeling he might be getting set up.

He stomped the feeling down.

Whether he was getting set up or not, the guy was offering him a way out and Buck had to admit he'd be stupid not to take it.

"Be careful with this weapon. It is a disintegration gun. Some of the guards wear them here now." He nodded at Buck's wounded shoulder. "You were lucky you came across a guard with the older model of weapon."

Buck nodded in full agreement. Better to feel pain than to be disintegrated.

"There is a guard right outside this door." Jarod continued. "The gun is set to kill. Just aim and pull the trigger."

They both tensed as the prison warden stirred briefly on the bed.

"I gather Virgin knows you're alive?" Buck asked quickly.

"She knows."

"I doubt it'll be easy to get her out of here without you. Are you sure you can't come with us? Isn't there a way I can get you out of here?"

Jarod looked down and Buck followed his gaze to the shiny gold anklet.

"If I leave this room without her permission I will be disintegrated by the drones. Believe me, sometimes I feel it would be easier to die that way, but I'm not a coward. I won't take the easy way out."

"Maybe we can jimmy the lock open?"

"It's state of the art. Voice activated by Cath. I have heard rumors there is a special salve that is also effective. Unfortunately I don't know which one."

"Jarod? Where are you, darling?" The prison warden's sleepy whisper curled through the semi-darkness.

"I'm here, Cath. I'm looking for something in the closet." He turned to Buck. "Wait until she's busy and then leave."

Buck nodded numbly and watched Jarod pad to the closet. He made a show of noise and then said rather seductively, "Ah, here is what I want. The whip."

Well that was appropriate, under the circumstances, Buck mused as he slouched into the shadows hoping the warden wouldn't see him.

He watched Jarod stride to the bedside where the prison warden lay stretched out and naked, eagerly awaiting the slave.

Mouth twisted in a grim smile, he quickly secured her wrists and ankles to the bedposts.

A moment later he brought down the whip upon the woman's breasts.

Cath whimpered beneath the onslaught.

"Harder, darling. Harder," she begged.

Buck frowned. The things a guy would do to protect his sister.

He wished he could somehow break Jarod out of here. But he didn't have the time or the resources. Jarod had urged him to hurry. His first priority lay with Virgin. He needed to get to her. Needed to see if she was okay.

Jarod let the whip fly again. It cracked against the warden's quivering stomach.

Buck flinched at the red welt that instantly appeared on her flesh and remembered the searing pain a similar whip had inflicted upon him when those blonde virgins had first captured him.

Oddly enough the passion poison had taken care of the whip pain on his body and if the warden spoke the truth, this Quick Healing Injection they'd given him would take care of the shoulder wound. Already he could feel the pain from the bullet wound had lessened substantially.

His grip tightened on the disintegration gun. The metal was smooth and warm in his hands. A grin cracked his lips. Cripes, it looked like one of those phasers from Star Trek.

His smile quickly disappeared and he frowned.

Star Trek was classic television. This was reality.

But would he be able to use this gun? Could he actually take a life?

In all his years of exploration, he'd never come up against hostiles. Heck, he'd never been on an inhabited planet before either.

But the thought of killing someone tonight sat heavy in his belly. His gaze drifted to the barred window. To the red-tinged moon.

His guts knotted with determination. He would spill blood if it meant saving the woman he loved.

The warden's moans grew louder and Buck clicked the door open a couple of inches and peered out.

A female guard stood right there in front of the door, her back to him.

He didn't miss the gun latched to a holster on her right hip. The gun looked exactly like the weapon Jarod had thrust into his hand.

A sick feeling clawed into Buck's belly

A disintegration gun.

From behind him the prison warden's moans grew even louder, more frantic, more desperate.

He knew he'd have to make his move within seconds and take advantage of what Jarod was doing to keep the warden distracted. He just wished he could figure out some way to free Jarod too.

Buck's hand tightened around the cool metal handle of the disintegration gun. The only thing that mattered right now was finding Virgin and getting out of this madhouse. Jarod would want what was best for his sister.

Aiming the gun at the guard's back, Buck closed his eyes and pulled the trigger. An odd strangled sound erupted from the guard and intermingled with the warden's moans.

Silence followed.

Buck froze.

Damn! Had the warden heard the odd sound?

He resisted the urge to look over his shoulder to see if the warden had seen him. Suddenly he heard a grunt from

Jarod. The sound was quickly followed by the warden's sensual moan.

Heart hammering violently in Buck's ears, he peered back out the door. The guard was gone.

Vanished.

Disintegrated.

Murdered by his hand.

Strangely enough, he didn't puke. Didn't freak out.

Relief was his only ally. The coast was now clear and Buck slipped out of the room.

Chapter Twelve

Virgin shivered inwardly as the prison doctor placed the golden clit and nipple rings on a velvety black cloth in front of Virgin.

"They're quite beautiful, aren't they?" the prison doctor said as she gazed down at the rings.

"Lovely," Virgin replied.

The doctor peered impatiently over her shoulder toward the open door. "I wonder what is taking Cath so long? She said she wanted to watch the insertion of the rings."

Virgin didn't say anything. She just wished the doctor would get all this over with because the instant she was free, she was taking off. She had to find Buck and Jarod and get them out of here. If getting fitted with mating rings was the quickest way out of this mess, she would do it.

"You don't know how lucky you are," the doctor cooed.

The harsh sound of chains rippled through the air as she lifted Virgin's right shackled ankle into a metal coupling strapped to the leg of the padded chair she'd been instructed to sit in.

"There's no need to tie me down. I can handle the pain." Virgin said.

"It's standard prison procedure," the prison doctor replied.

Virgin stifled a surge of panic as the metal band snapped cool against her skin. The doctor clamped it shut. She did the same with the other ankle and then released the manacles that the guards had shackled her with when they'd moved her from the cell.

The doctor straightened herself and smiled warmly at Virgin.

"It isn't everyday an escaped Death Row convict gets a second chance at life. You must have done something right to stay in Cath's favor."

The doctor placed Virgin's right wrist upon the padded armrest of the chair and clamped the cool metal band around her wrist, just above her shackle.

Great. Just great, she thought solemnly.

She was exchanging one set of shackles for another. She didn't like this helpless feeling of being tied down and at the mercy of Cath.

A strong surge of changing her mind about accepting the mating rings swamped Virgin, but she clamped down on the powerful feeling.

She had to go through with this insane fiasco. It was her only way out.

"I tried my best to fall into her favors." The prison doctor continued chatting as she gazed longingly at the rings. "Thought I'd be lucky to get an extension on my life if I could get her interested in me. Unfortunately Cath has already signed my death warrant."

Virgin shivered at the woman's words. A woman with a signed death warrant meant she'd revealed to the hub she had entered menopause. She would be useless to the hub, of non-child bearing age, not eligible for any prison sentences if she did anything wrong. It meant she only had a few weeks to get her affairs in order before she was executed.

"Have you thought about running?" Virgin asked, trying to keep her mind off what the doctor was about to do to her.

"And go where? The Outer Limits? There's nothing out there but sand and monsters. Besides, if I were to run, I'd only end up like you were, a fugitive. That's no way to live."

"You'd be free."

The doctor made a funny strangled laugh. "How can one be free with the entire population of Paradise hunting one down? Besides, freedom is just a word, Virgin. Just a word."

"For a long time I thought it was just a word too, doc."

The doctor's head snapped up at Virgin's soft words. Her eyes narrowed with disgust.

"You've always been such a dreamer, Virgin. Always spouting off about giving males better conditions, providing them with basic education and who knows what else is lurking around in the back of your mind."

"I believe in allowing a woman to die naturally and not being murdered simply because she can't produce babies anymore."

The doctor sucked in a sharp breath as if Virgin had punched her right in the stomach.

"Talk like that will get you into the same troubles as you had the past year. It's best you just be Cath's mate and forget the rest of your nonsense."

Virgin winced inwardly as the prison doctor fastened the last metal band over Virgin's wrist and undid her other shackles.

Then she headed toward the door. "I'm going to see what is taking Cath so long. Be back in a minute." The doctor said as she left the room and closed the door.

Virgin cursed softly beneath her breath as she heard the electronic lock snap into place. She didn't know why she was so angry. She wasn't going anywhere. Not with these metal clamps securing her in much the same way they'd chained her when she'd given birth to her male child four months ago.

Virgin frowned when she remembered how she'd hated being sentenced to a male child. And she'd hated it even more when she'd been told her first session with the fucking machine had been a success.

For nine long months she'd carried hate in her heart for the male child buried inside her womb. But the hate had disappeared during the several hours of excruciating birth pain.

At the first sight of the blond-haired blue-eyed male child, the deepest, warmest feeling had swamped her emotions. It was a powerful feeling she'd never experienced in her life. A feeling she hadn't been able to put a name to, even to this very day.

And now it made her sad to think of what the women of Paradise had lost because she'd educated Jarod when she was younger. She should have known something like that would come back to haunt her and ruin her plans.

But she'd wanted her twin to know there was more to life than being a sex slave.

If she had to do it over again, she would.

Besides, if it hadn't been the excuse of her educating Jarod, they would have come up with something else to get her out of the way.

The prison doctor's attitude was a prime example of why she'd wanted to help the women of Paradise. It was another one of the reasons she'd fought so hard to become a Queen and then a High Queen. The doctor was a woman who was a few weeks away from her death appointment and she'd simply accepted her fate. She was a woman who didn't believe in freedom or living as long as possible without being put down simply because she was menopausal.

Virgin had wanted to change the laws but she hadn't realized she would encounter such opposition to her ideas. Hadn't comprehended they could set her up so easily and take her down so quickly all because of her compassion for her twin.

She remembered the shocked look on all their faces at the council meeting when she'd put forth her proposal of allowing the women in prison to take care of their own children, both the males and the females, until the age of three years instead of two months before having them removed from the women. It would allow the children to have access to the nutrients found in the breast milk instead of forcing the women to sit idly in their prison cells, their breast milk drying up and having virtually nothing else to do but work in the gardens, kitchen, laundry and other tasks while the Nurturers fed artificially created milk to the babies.

Many babies' lives were lost due to allergic reactions to the artificial milk. Her proposal would save the Hub some lives and also save many credits by not having to hire Nurturers for the first three years of a child's life because the prison women would take care of them.

Accompanying her proposal, Virgin had presented research that she'd discovered in the Caves of Knowledge. Research by their ancestors who had proven that nutrients in the mother's milk created smarter and healthier offspring, that a baby needed to bond with its bearer in order to gain confidence and self-esteem at an early age.

She'd even presented her own childhood feelings to the group, feelings of wanting more from the Nurturers and Educators, feelings of wanting to belong to someone but never being fulfilled with the revolving doors of new faces in the Nurturers and Educators every few weeks.

Her childhood had been lonely and she'd found solace only in other female children who had expressed similar feelings, many of whose sobs Virgin had used as a lullaby to fall asleep in the cold, sterile environment they'd all been raised in.

She swore she'd seen a tear or two in a couple of the High Queen eyes, especially in the red-haired Jasmine's eyes, the High Queen, who after the initial shocks of Virgin's presentation, had seemed quiet and thoughtful instead of participating in the heated out-of-control debate that had followed that day.

It had been High Queen Jasmine who'd also helped Virgin escape from prison and had subsequently freed Virgin's friend, Queen Jacey and the talking man Ben when they, too, had been captured by the new self-proclaimed Queen Cath and thrown into prison.

Virgin had studied Jacey and Ben before their capture. Had noticed the closeness between the male and the Queen. Had watched the male break down her barriers.

Had spied in stunned fascination as Jacey had allowed the talking male to fuck her in illegal positions while bound in a slave cabin. The excruciating pleasure he'd brought to her with his healthy shaft and the camaraderie between the two, had left Virgin desperately craving the same for herself.

She'd wanted her own male, a male who looked at her as if she were special. A male who'd looked at her the same way as Buck had looked at her before she'd betrayed him.

Virgin closed her eyes at the thought of Buck.

What where they doing to him right now? What was he thinking? Was he cursing her? Was he wishing he'd never come for her?

The sound of the door lock being slipped open, made Virgin tense.

"Ah, here she is. All ready to accept my rings." Cath's voice boomed ultra-sweet through the sterile room making Virgin instantly aware something was wrong.

She noticed the worried look on the doctor's face as she quickly passed Virgin and headed into a nearby alcove. She observed the way Cath's lips were tight, as if she were angry.

Despite her mounting fear, she forced herself to face Cath and smile. It was the hardest thing she'd ever had to do in her life, next to betraying Buck, of course.

"Yes, I'm ready to accept your rings, Cath," she replied, surprised at how steady her voice sounded under the circumstances.

Cath smiled over sweetly and continued to stare at the mating rings on the table.

"I just left your twin, Virgin. Left him to his punishment."

Virgin's smile dropped. Her heart picked up a violent pace.

"Apparently during the time he was pleasuring me, he let your talking male loose."

Oh Goddess of Freedom!

Buck was free.

"Don't look so happy, Virgin. He will be caught and dealt with swiftly. Perhaps I'll administer the same punishment as I've given Jarod?"

Icy terror made Virgin dizzy. "What have you done to him?"

"He's been sentenced to twenty-four hours of ball weights. Quite heavy ones I might add. He's had that punishment many times before. He's quite docile and sensitive after that. But of course, that's only the beginning of his punishment this time. I haven't figured out what to do to him next. Perhaps more whippings? Although his body is already frightfully scarred from them, he might not feel the full extent of the pain. Perhaps I'll gouge out his other eye? He really doesn't need to see anyway. His other senses will take over in pleasuring me."

"You do anything to Jarod and our deal is off," Virgin warned and instinctively pulled against her restraints.

"I thought you might say that. So I've decided to punish you too."

Why wasn't she surprised? Cath had always loved to torment her. Why would now be any different?

"Doctor! Get in here with that item I requested!" Cath snapped.

A cold shiver of fear shuddered up Virgin's spine when the doctor quickly entered the room carrying a poker. The end glowed a bright orange.

What in the world was Cath up to?

"Perhaps I'll gouge out your eye instead of Jarod's? I'd have a matching set of lovers," she chuckled.

Panic slammed into her like a bolt of lightning. She closed her eyes and twisted her head away.

Her wrists and ankles pulled fruitlessly at her restraints in a desperate effort to break free.

Cath grinned, getting off on her terror.

Bile rose in her throat. She fought it back down.

"How about I brand your beautifully silky breast?"

Unbearable heat washed against the top curve of her right breast. She tried to push herself away but the chair stopped her cold.

"Now think about this, Cath. Do you really want to mark me?" Despite her attempt she couldn't stop the shakiness from showing in her voice.

Cath's grin widened. The heated end of the poker drew perilously close to her skin.

Thankfully, she halted the disfiguring weapon about an inch away.

"Y'know, you are so right. I really prefer not to see charred skin while I fuck you senseless."

The heat of the poker drew away from her breast and Virgin closed her eyes and exhaled a sigh of relief.

"I think I'd prefer it right here."

Before she could make sense of Cath's words, a burning pain unlike anything she'd ever experienced sliced into the muscular curve of her left hip.

Chapter Thirteen

Virgin's agonizing scream shot straight through Buck's body, jolting every single nerve and making him freeze where he stood just outside Jarod's cell. Her tormented yell drifted off into silence.

Buck's hands dampened with sweat and his heart slammed against his heart like a battering ram. Disjointed images raced through his mind as to what had made her scream that way.

All his instincts begged him to run. To find her. To comfort her.

But he forced himself to open Jarod's cell door and step inside.

"What are you doing? I've already told you to forget about me. Get Virgin!" Jarod's panicked whisper almost made Buck turn away. Almost made him run blindly into the halls.

But he couldn't. He'd seen the guards drag Jarod back to his cell. It had taken a while for them to leave and when they had, Buck had been able to flip the switch in the Security room and hurried back to Jarod.

"Forget me. Save Virgin!" Jarod urged in a pain-racked whisper from the dark depths of his cell.

"Her cell is empty," he explained as he located the sex slave. "I don't know where she is. I need your help. You know this place better than I do. We can get to her quicker if you lead the way."

Buck swallowed back a grimace when he noted Jarod's naked body shackled to the stone wall. Jarod's arms were up stretched tight and secured by heavy chains, his legs widespread and secured in the same way. And he sure didn't miss the heavy metal weights dangling off Jarod's swollen balls.

With trembling fingers, Buck managed to free Jarod from all his restraints.

The one-eyed sex slave slumped to his knees. His eyes were tightly closed and he winced with every breath.

"You okay?" Buck asked, hoping to hell the man was up to helping him find Virgin.

He tried hard not to think of what had caused Virgin to scream like that. Tried hard not to scream in anger and frustration himself.

"Where do you think her scream came from?" Buck asked as Jarod suddenly ripped the disintegration gun out of his hands and rose shakily to his feet.

"I'm not sure."

"You think they were outfitting her with those rings?" Buck asked hopefully. Nipple and clit rings could be removed. Wounds healed.

"I don't think so."

"I was afraid you'd say that."

As they slipped out of the cool cell and into the hallway, he didn't have the heart to ask what Jarod thought they were doing to her. Especially when he noted the grim line to his mouth.

Rage soared inside him and Buck found it hard to think straight. His stomach twisted with nausea and the bullet wound in his shoulder throbbed painfully. He was going to kill that prison warden. So help him he was going to murder anyone who had touched Virgin.

A gentle pat on Buck's back made him jump.

Jarod smiled shakily. "Virgin is tough. She's a High Queen. Torture was part of her Queen training. She can handle whatever they inflict upon her."

She'd been tortured? Great. How many times? Why hadn't she told him?

God! He'd tied her up. Practically forced himself upon her.

The sickness rolling in his gut notched up a degree.

It was all his fault she was back here. If he'd been smart in the first place, the virgins wouldn't have captured him, the passion poison wouldn't have infected him and she wouldn't have rescued him.

They might never have met.

He would never have known the sultry seductress. Or experienced the happiness that continued to flood his heart whenever he thought of her.

He'd take her home with him. He'd show her that Earth was a better environment for their kids, for her baby.

Man, he would be a great father to her child. He could teach the kid how to fish, play baseball…

Without warning, pain exploded in his wounded shoulder as Jarod crashed into him knocking him full force against the wall. Blackness hovered at the edges of his sight but he sure as heck didn't miss the green beam of light from a disintegration beam zip past where he'd been standing a split second ago.

Jarod had just saved his life!

Pointing his gun at the guard firing at them, Jarod returned fire.

The green light zeroed in on her forehead. Her cry of pain was muffled as she disappeared in a puff of green smoke.

Buck shook his head, trying to clear the silver stars dancing frantically in front of his eyes. Warmth flooded his shoulder. He didn't have to look down to know he was bleeding again.

"You okay?" Jarod asked, concern splashing against his face.

"I'll live. Thanks for getting me out of the way. I owe you one."

"We're even. That was the security guard. When she doesn't report back to Cath soon, there's going to be trouble. In the meantime we're going to cause some trouble of our own."

Jarod entered the same room Buck had been in earlier. The Security room. Three walls were covered with an abundance of computer screens surveying the naked prisoners in their cells, or spying on women working in the laundry or kitchen.

Jared began flipping the top line of black switches.

"What are you doing?"

"Releasing the prisoners."

Buck couldn't help but grin. "Of course. Diversionary tactic."

He joined Jarod at the console and began flipping the next row of switches.

A minute later they could hear shrieks from women who couldn't believe their good luck as they quickly erupted from their cells.

"They should stop Cath in her tracks," Jarod grinned as he began on another row of switches.

"How do you know about all this? The switches and the Security room?"

"Cath likes to show off her prison. Loves to get fucked in different rooms. I used the fucking tours to gather information so I could set the women free one day. Looks like today is their day."

The sounds of the combined panic and excitement grew louder and they watched as women began rushing past the open doorway to the Security room. Most held blossoming bellies as they ran naked down the hallway. A couple looked as if they were ready to give birth right now.

"The guards will start shooting soon. That's when we make our move."

Anger zapped a fresh dose of reality through Buck.

"We can't let them shoot the women!"

"The guards will use the stun guns. The women are too valuable. As you can see most are carrying future sex slaves and workers."

"Still, someone can get seriously hurt!"

"It's a chance I'm willing to take to help Virgin, aren't you?"

The challenge in his voice sobered Buck.

Jarod was right. They had to stall whatever was happening to Virgin. However, it didn't mean he had to like this diversion. And he sure didn't like this planet. It was screwy. Out of whack. But it wasn't up to him to enforce his beliefs on these people. He was supposed to be following NASA's protocol. Supposed to be keeping a low profile and secretly study the planet and the inhabitants, not getting involved with the first woman who saved his life. And he sure wasn't supposed to kill people in a fit of rage because the woman he loved was in danger.

Uh oh. The love word again.

Panic-stricken screams emerged from somewhere nearby, breaking Buck from his thoughts.

"The guards are shooting. Let's go!" Jarod shouted.

Stumbling behind the sex slave, Buck followed him into the crowded hallway. Some of the women screamed in terror at seeing the two males on the loose. Most were in too much of a hurry finding a way out and ignored Buck and Jarod.

Hot swollen bellies pressed against him as he fought to keep up to Jarod. His injured shoulder got jarred over and over again. Pain soon became his constant companion. In order to dim the agony, he thought of Virgin.

Remembered the sweet surprise swamping her face when he'd entered her hot channel the very first time.

As far as he was concerned she had been a virgin. He'd been her first man.

The women accompanying his brothers, Ben and Joe, had explained about the fucking machines and how they impregnated the prisoners. Those machines didn't count.

He had been her first and there was something honorable about that.

The fact that she'd dragged him to her secret hideout knowing full well that he was infected with a potent sex drug, knowing full well that she could have traded him for her baby and allowed Cath to cure him, made him believe she'd wanted to get fucked. That she'd wanted to experience the sexual connection between a man and a woman. In the end, she'd wanted more than just betraying him.

The look of love and trust shining in her eyes when he'd taken her sweet cunt into his mouth, and then again when he'd tied her to the bed and bound her breasts, hadn't been faked.

And the look of guilt, the look of pain searing across her face when she thought she'd betrayed him by lying about his brothers being held at prison hadn't been phony either.

She carried a lot of emotions in her heart for him. Just as he did for her.

Emotions that needed to be explored.

He couldn't wait to see her again. Couldn't wait to wrap his arms around her hot body and tell her he loved her.

He couldn't wait to…

"She's in there. The doctor's office." Jarod indicated an open doorway. "I'll stay here and stand guard. Go!"

Buck stepped into the doorway and froze.

Sweet mercy!

Virgin sat naked on an odd-looking contraption of a chair. Her face sickly pale and twisted in pain. Her eyes were scrunched closed. Her chest heaved with steady tortured breaths.

And that's when he smelled it.

The sickening stench of burned flesh.

Virgin's flesh.

The sight of the ugly burn mark etched into the curve of her right hip made his stomach roll. For a second he thought he just might pass out.

He didn't.

The burn was two inches long and just as wide.

An ugly red.

A brand with the letter C.

He didn't know how long he stood there in the doorway, riveted by the brand.

But when his gaze lifted he looked straight into a pair of pain-glazed blue eyes.

"Buck? You came for me?"

Surprise etched her hoarse voice and Buck couldn't understand why she wouldn't expect him to come for her.

From behind him, Jarod began shooting, urging Buck into action.

"Where's the prison warden?" he asked as he quickly unsnapped her metal cuffs.

She nodded toward an open door at the back of the room.

"They went that way as soon as they realized the prisoners were loose."

"It leads to the tunnels. You'll never find them down there," Jarod yelled through the doorway as Buck draped a sheet around her shivering body.

"So they've escaped." Anger snapped inside him at having missed his chance at killing the bitch.

"Buck, where's the baby?"

"He's safe with my brothers. C'mon, let's get out of here. Lean on me," he instructed.

She did as he asked, her hand curling around his shoulder, her teeth gritted against the pain that must be firing up her side from that brand.

"The doctor keeps her guns in the top drawer in the far corner over there," Jarod yelled as he continued to fire from the doorway. "I could use a little help here!"

"Stay here." Buck said as he stumbled toward where Jarod had indicated.

"Are you kidding? I want in on the action too," Virgin said.

She joined Buck where he retrieved the weapons.

Concern ripped through her voice as she examined the blood leaking from his shoulder wound. "You look about ready to drop. Are you all right?"

"I'll be fine," Buck grinned. "As long as we're together."

Her answering smile gave him a much-needed shot of adrenaline that deadened the pain in his shoulder.

Joining Jarod at the door, Buck took aim. Careful not to hit the prisoners who rushed past, he nailed a guard right in the chest. She didn't utter a sound as she disintegrated.

"Good shot," Jarod praised.

Buck wished he could take satisfaction at the killing but it just didn't sit right aiming a gun at someone, pulling the trigger and watching them disappear into thin air. He much preferred the old-fashioned way of seeing a body. At least then there was a chance the person wasn't dead.

He peeked at Virgin who'd taken a position between him and Jarod. "Y'know if we ever get out of here—"

She stopped him cold by pressing a finger to his lips. "*When* we get out of here."

"I like your scenario better. When we get out of here, I'm going to show you just how much I love you."

A green line slammed off the doorjamb urging them to return fire. The guard disappeared in a green haze.

"How the hell many of these guards are there in this building?" Buck asked.

"Too many," Jarod replied. "I think the way is clear now. I'll lead."

Buck nodded.

Grabbing Virgin's hand, he followed Jarod and merged once again with the frantic prisoners.

They encountered no more guards over the next few minutes and to his surprise the halls quickly became deserted.

Buck was about to breathe a sigh of relief that maybe, just maybe, they might get out of there without anymore trouble when another volley of gunshots erupted right in front of them. An unarmed guard came flying around the corner and ran screaming toward the trio.

Fear blazed in her eyes.

From behind her, Buck noticed Jacey turn the corner.

She took aim and fired.

The guard moaned and dropped to the hallway, motionless. A large pool of blood blossomed across her upper back.

When she spied Buck and Virgin she smiled. "I much prefer the disintegration gun. No mess to clean up."

"Looks like the cavalry has arrived," Buck mumbled.

A split second later darkness enveloped him.

* * * * *

"What happened?" Ben and Joe both chorused, faces full of concern as they joined Virgin, Jarod and Jacey who hovered beside Buck's unconscious body.

"He was shot earlier. He's lost a lot of blood," Virgin replied shakily.

Her heart hammered insanely against her chest as she quickly ripped a piece off the sheet Buck had used to wrap around her nude body. Balling up the material she pressed it against the hole in his shoulder that now oozed blood.

When she'd seen him collapse, Virgin's heart had squeezed so tightly she thought she would pass out from the overwhelming fear that he might be dead.

Thankfully Jacey did what she couldn't bring herself to do and checked his pulse.

"He's alive. The bullet wound doesn't look bad. He'll be fine. Probably fainted due to the loss of blood," Jacey said and Virgin found herself sighing with relief.

"He was given a Quick Healing Injection but I pushed him against the wall when he was in the line of fire. I'm afraid his shoulder was re-injured."

"Who are you?" Joe said as Ben ripped the gun out of Jarod's hand.

"He's my twin. He's helping us," Virgin explained. "Where's Annie? She's a doctor. She can help Buck."

"She's taking care of the kid back at camp," Ben said as he and Joe grabbed Buck beneath his armpits and hoisted his unconscious figure to his feet. "We figured it was safest to keep the doctor out of harm's way. Now we just have to get Buck to her."

"I'll clear the way up ahead." Jacey said. "Virgin, you come along with us. I'm sure Buck will want to talk with you when he wakes up." Without waiting for an answer she took off at a dead run.

"She'll catch up in a minute," Jarod said.

When the others were out of earshot, Jarod spoke. "This is where we say goodbye."

"No way! I want you to come with me."

"I cannot." His gaze lowered to the golden anklet clamped around his ankle.

"I can get you out of those. There's a special salve. I know where it is kept. "

He grinned and his shoulders slumped with relief. "I was hoping you'd say that."

Grabbing his hand she led him down the hallway.

A few minutes later they slipped into the deserted prison warden's office.

Within minutes, Virgin had found the special salve and stuck some into the lock on Jarod's anklet.

The lock instantly popped open.

With shaking fingers, Jarod unclasped the hideous device and held it up, staring at it with his one eye. "This has kept me hostage for more than a year. Hand me your disintegration gun."

Virgin handed it to him and watched as he laid the gold anklet onto the ground, aimed and pulled the trigger. A split second later the anklet disappeared.

He smiled wearily. "Now we say goodbye."

"Please come with me," Virgin said, totally prepared to beg. She hadn't seen him in so long that she never wanted him out of her sight again.

"I see the way the one called Buck looks at you. He wants you. He will keep you safe. I, on the other hand, have revenge in my heart. I cannot rest until I kill Cath and some of the others. She's the one who had me tortured. She's the one who made me confess that you educated me and then lie about you educating the other slaves." Jarod frowned. "She did it by brainwashing me, injecting me with powerful drugs. And she did it with the blessing of three of the High Fives. I must find my friends Taylor and Blackie in The Outer Limits. We will regroup. Then I will come back to exact my revenge against Cath and the others. Perhaps we will try again to free more male sex slaves in other hubs."

"If you haven't heard from them, maybe Blackie and Taylor are dead by now. Many of the escaped slaves were severely injured when the army came in that day."

"That is true. But I must know for sure. They may have been recaptured. Either way I must know their fate."

A sudden noise from behind them made the siblings turn to see Jacey standing in the doorway with an overfilled knapsack. Obviously she'd been busy raiding the prison.

"Looks like the building's been deserted. The prisoners are all gone. All the babies and children too, even the guards. Joe, Ben and Buck are heading back to camp. Are you coming?" she asked both of them.

Virgin looked at her twin hoping he might change his mind.

He shook his head.

Suddenly she felt torn.

Should she go with Buck? Or retrieve her baby and go with Jarod and help him free more slaves?

"Go," he whispered. "Be with the talking male and your baby. At least then I will be able to concentrate on my mission without worrying about you."

Tears blurred her vision as she made her decision. She nodded agreement.

Jarod wrapped his strong arms around her and gave her an affectionate hug.

"Be safe," he said.

Without another word he brushed past Jacey.

And then he was gone.

Chapter Fourteen

Three days had passed since they'd all escaped from the prison. Jacey had led Virgin to a camp where both she and Buck were now mending quite nicely thanks to the Quick Healing Injections Annie had given them.

However, mixed emotions were her constant companion.

A sharp happiness clung to her at having her sweet baby boy back in her arms. Yet her happiness was overshadowed by the loss of her twin, Jarod, and also by Buck's jovial attitude.

He hadn't mentioned her betrayal of him. Hadn't mentioned the ugly scar Cath had branded into the side of her hip.

Nor had he attempted to have any type of physical contact with her.

He was acting as if he hadn't said that he would show her how much he loved her while they'd been pinned under fire in the prison.

He was acting as if she were some special friend and nothing more.

And yet she ached to be more to him than just a friend.

Much more.

* * * * *

"Annie? Can I talk to you for a minute?" Virgin asked when she finally found Annie alone in the camp.

The doctor looked up from the carrots she'd been slicing for supper.

"Sure, what's up?"

"Annie, I…I think I'm pregnant."

"Join the club."

Virgin blinked at Annie's unexpected announcement.

Annie laughed. "Don't look so surprised. We're women, that's what happens when we mate with a male without protection, as you very well know."

"You've told Joe?"

"I took the test the other day. Last night I told Joe. Didn't you notice the big smile on his face this morning?"

"He always has a big smile on his face when he looks at you." Virgin laughed.

Annie got a dreamy look on her face. "We keep each other happy. I bet you want me to give you a pregnancy test, don't you?"

"Please. I need to know. Although…" Virgin patted her abdomen. "I have this odd feeling that I am. I just want it confirmed."

"Well as you know, our modern technology where pregnancy is considered allows a woman to know if she's pregnant within hours of conception. It just so happens I have more pregnancy kits. I asked Jacey if she got the chance to get some medical supplies from the prison Doctor's office while she and the others were in the prison looking for you. I'm sure she'll be wanting a pregnancy test one of these days too." Annie winked at her cheerfully. "Don't worry. We'll find out within minutes if you're pregnant and how far along you are. How's that?"

"It sounds perfect. Thank you."

"I'll get a kit and a container for you to pee in."

While Annie hurried over to the tattered knapsack that Jacey had carried out of the prison, Virgin hugged herself with both dread and happiness.

Could she actually be pregnant? And what if she was? What should she do?

All this was so unfamiliar to her. Being alone. Having a baby to take care of. Being pregnant yet again.

She'd been raised to the fact that only imprisoned women were allowed to become pregnant and she'd been taught that the Nurturers were supposed to take care of the baby, not her.

And yet she hadn't been able to leave her own baby in the prison. From the moment she'd discovered him missing from her cell, she'd only thought of escaping and finding a way of getting him back. She hadn't given much thought to how she would care for him or that she could get pregnant while fucking Buck.

Oh Goddess of Freedom! What should she do?

* * * * *

"Is it true? Are you pregnant?"

Virgin swirled around at the sound of Joe's strangled voice.

His question made her wish she hadn't wandered so far away from camp in order to digest the news that Annie had confirmed she was pregnant.

She didn't think Joe would hurt her. But he'd always seemed cold toward her. Cold and aloof.

For an educated male, an outsider, he knew nothing of the ways of her people and so she supposed Joe would be upset with her regarding what had been forced upon him in prison.

"I'm sorry to disturb you but I saw you leave camp earlier and I saw Annie hide the pregnancy kit. I put two and two together. Is it true? Are you pregnant with my child?"

Oh no! He didn't know! Didn't have a clue at what lengths she'd gone to in prison in order to prevent pregnancy in herself and the other woman.

"There's something I need to explain to you," Virgin said quickly, eagerly wanting to rid the anguish bruising his face.

"If you're going to tell me that you're pregnant because of us being hooked up together to the prison fucking machine, I'll do right by you. I'll make sure you and the baby are well taken care of."

"The baby isn't yours. None of the women in Cell Block C are pregnant by your seed."

Confusion flooded his features. "I don't understand. "

"It's well-known that I don't agree with some of the laws of my people. It's why I fought so hard to become a High Queen. Only High Queens can change the laws. I wanted to change them, especially the ones that force women to become pregnant against their will. But then last year I was sent to prison and immediately impregnated.

When I gave birth I knew it would be only a matter of time before they came for me again. I had to find some way to stop what was going to happen." She continued. "In the prison yard I was able to secretly collect wild carrot seeds and several other herbs that when mixed together and eaten will prevent a woman from becoming pregnant. During the last two months of my stay at the prison, I was secretly placing these herbs into the prison women's food supply while I was assigned to kitchen duty. As a result no woman became pregnant by your sperm."

Joe reached up and stroked his chin thoughtfully.

"Yet this morning you took a pregnancy test. You don't have to lie to spare me, Virgin."

"I'm not lying, Joe. The child is Buck's. After escaping the prison, I had no reason to keep taking the herbs. And when I rescued Buck, I didn't have time to think, let alone take the herbs. I just knew I needed him alive and then everything just happened so fast and…"

Virgin stopped talking when she noticed amusement sparkling in his green eyes. It was the first time he'd ever smiled at her and it felt good to know he wasn't mad at her anymore.

"And now you have feelings for Buck?"

Virgin nodded.

"Have you told him about us? About what happened in the prison?" he asked.

"I'd rather not."

Joe fell silent for a minute and then nodded. "Okay, he won't hear it from me."

"Hear what from you?"

Before she could turn around, Buck's solid arms wrapped snugly around her waist. She couldn't help but tremble with need as the hot length of his swollen cock pressed intimately against the crack in her ass.

"Virgin would prefer to tell you herself." Joe winked at her. "I'm heading back to the campsite. You have the place to enjoy all by yourselves. See you later."

"Tell me what?" he whispered again when Joe had gone.

Virgin turned her head and kissed him.

His lips were smooth and hot beneath her onslaught. He groaned as her mouth opened and she darted her tongue into his hot inviting mouth. Their tongues clashed and slid against each other in an erotic dance. Liquid heat erupted between her legs, her breasts swelled with arousal and her nipples became inflamed with need.

Virgin whimpered beneath the beautiful sensations.

He broke the kiss.

His hoarse breath licked like tiny flames of fire against her skin as he nuzzled his mouth to her neck.

"Don't worry too much about Jarod. He seems to be able to take care of himself."

"I know. It's just that I wanted to have him near me. Wanted to find out what happened to him over the past year."

"I'm under the impression he wouldn't want to discuss it with you, Virgin," Buck said as he caressed her chin tenderly.

"You're probably right. But still I just found him again and now he's gone."

"Did he say where he was headed?"

"Into the Outer Limits to search for two of his friends. I hope he'll be all right."

"He's a survivor, Virgin. He told me he could have taken the easy way out many times and gotten himself killed by the drones, but he didn't do it. He let the women out of their cells the first chance he got and now he's gone looking for his friends. He strikes me as the type who wants to help others."

Virgin smiled, suddenly feeling a whole lot better. "That's what he told me."

"You see. He'll be fine. And now back to us. What is it that you wanted to tell me?"

"That I have feelings for you. Wonderful feelings I've never felt before for anyone."

His sharp inhalation and the way his lips curled against her flesh made Virgin realize he was pleased with her words.

"I was under the impression things like that didn't occur around these parts," he teased.

His hands settled upon the curves of her hips and he pressed his cock harder against the crack in her ass.

Virgin shivered with anticipation. "This is the first time you've touched me since…"

"Since we got free?"

Virgin nodded. "I thought maybe you didn't want me anymore because of the brand and because of what I did to you, betraying you."

He chuckled against her neck.

"What's so funny?"

"I didn't come near you because I thought I might hurt myself."

"What do you mean? I'd never hurt you. Not on purpose. Not anymore."

"It had nothing to do with you. I had to make sure I was well enough to perform properly. Now that Annie fixed up my shoulder I feel a whole hell of a lot better. So much in fact that I want to show you exactly how much I love you like I promised back there in prison."

Virgin swallowed her excitement. Love. It was a forbidden word among her people. But by the intense desire in his voice when he spoke of it, it was something very valuable to him. And whatever he valued she would too.

"You really love me?"

"I wouldn't have come back for you in that prison if I didn't."

His hands slid from her waist. She inhaled sharply as his hot fingers curled over the thin fabric of her shorts.

"As for you betraying me? I think I have sufficient punishment in store for you." The soft way he said it made heated blood course through her veins.

Mild air blew against her ass as he slipped her clothing down her hips allowing her a moment to step out of it.

"Now bend over and spread your legs. Honey, I'm going to show you exactly how much I love you and exactly what the punishment is."

Oh Goddess of Freedom! He was going to take her from behind!

"Hold your ankles with your hands." His words dripped with heat encouraging Virgin to do as he asked.

She bent over at the waist. Tangling her trembling fingers around her bare ankles, she eagerly awaited her punishment.

A hot hand slid between her legs and her cunt screamed for joy as he began to massage her clitoris. The pleasure he created was wonderful, the heat from his hand intense and quite arousing.

She couldn't stop herself from moaning out loud.

"Easy, Virgin, I haven't even started yet," he laughed.

"You best get to it then," she breathed with a sudden impatience. She ached to be filled with his hard flesh. Ached to have his cock thrusting into her in an uncontrollable dance. Wanted desperately to be his woman.

A sharp smack against her left ass cheek made her cry out in surprise.

"What was that for?" she gasped.

"Just a little prelude of your punishment."

Another blow heated her right ass cheek.

"Buck what are you doing?" If he thought spanking her was going to be her punishment he was seriously mistaken.

"I've been wanting to do this all day. Indulge me. I'll make it worth your while."

Another smack quickly followed. The fiery heat spread through her ass cheeks and into her lower belly, making her gasp in shock.

The finger rubbing her swollen clitoris increased in speed along with the pleasure. A large hot finger suddenly impaled her.

With a strangled moan she writhed against the unexpected pleasure shooting like lightning up her vagina.

He chuckled softly. "You're already soaked down here. I'm glad to see my spanking pleases you."

He withdrew his finger and a hand slid a scorching trail over the curves of her blistering ass cheeks with such a gentle caress that Virgin quivered beneath his soft touch. The pressure against her clitoris increased to a higher degree and the storm building deep inside her roared to life.

Perspiration broke out all over her.

She inhaled ragged breaths at his next words.

"Your shapely ass is so hot and so pink, so silky smooth."

His fingers slid lower and inward.

Her eyes widened as his long fingers speared her ass cheeks apart. Holding her breath, she forced herself to relax and he was able to slip inside her anal channel.

Her muscles clenched tightly against his sensual insertion. The position of his finger felt so good as he massaged tenderly inside, preparing her for his entry. Slowly he slid out, but before he totally withdrew he slammed his finger deep inside her ass again. A rush of pleasure pain made her wince. It quickly disintegrated as his finger began a seductive thrust in and out of her like a miniature cock.

A second and then a third finger penetrated her.

By the time he was finished preparing Virgin, her legs were trembling and the arousal was screaming through her in a fever pitch.

When the head of his swollen cock slid smoothly into her cunt instead of her ass, she was slightly disappointed. She'd wanted to experience more of those wonderful sensations in her ass.

Perhaps this was another phase of her punishment? Keeping her off balance?

He drove his cock deep into her cunt in one violent thrust making her inhale sharply.

Closing her eyes she gave into the wonderful fullness his thick rod created as he slid in and out of her wet vagina in torturously slow strokes. Her hands tightened on her ankles as riotous desire screamed through her soaked vagina.

Suddenly he withdrew and pressed the thick bulging head of his cock between her ass cheeks.

Finally! He was finally going to impale her ass with his cock.

Suddenly she remembered his cock was much bigger than the dildo he'd used when he'd double-penetrated her back at the shelter.

Would she be able to handle his size?

A slither of fear tingled up her spine as he slowly pushed inside.

The pressure of his thickness in her ass was strange.

A finger slid against her clit once again. The arousing sensations brought her quickly to the edge of a climax. But he wouldn't let her explode. Wouldn't allow her to dive into the inferno threatening to claim her.

He was a master at pleasure. Knowing exactly when to back off in order to prevent her from achieving satisfaction.

She writhed in agony at the denial of fulfillment, becoming flushed with desire, her mind tense with anticipation.

She moaned out her protest as he continued to glide his cock in and out of her ass in achingly slow thrusts. He was going too slow. Not deep enough.

She wanted to be fucked harder, deeper, rougher. Wanted relief from this throbbing need he created that left her gasping and whimpering.

This must be part of his punishment for her. But how long would he keep her hovering at the edge before he would give her the satisfaction she craved?

He eased his cock deeper into her ass, burying himself halfway.

Finally!

Her anal muscles tightened around the thick intrusion, making him groan with pleasure. He probed deeper into her while his finger began a frenzied rubbing against her swollen clit. A finger slipped inside her soaked vagina making it harder for Virgin to keep holding onto her ankles. Each penetration into her anus became deeper, more filling, driving her closer toward that something wild she craved.

Automatically her hips pumped backwards, encouraging him to bring her to full satisfaction.

"You seem to be ready to have the final phase of your punishment administered." Buck chuckled.

He speared his cock deeper into her ass. The length and pressure of his hot flesh sinking into her was almost unbearable. The pain was both beautiful and dangerous as it intermingled with the scorching pleasure.

His hips pumped faster. His hard balls slapped against her flesh. Perspiration beaded her. His fingers moved frantically against her sensitive clit.

She was going to climax any second!

Her instincts kicked in and she thrust her hips back full force, meeting his every violent plunge. His cock seemed to be on fire as he impaled her over and over again.

The pace of his thrusts grew more determined. More fierce.

It pushed her over the edge.

Throwing her head back she cried out as exquisite agony burst like a dark tornado straight though her lower belly. Both her vaginal and anal muscles spasmed in a magnificent rhythm.

His long hot cock continued to stretch and fill her with his solid swift thrusts. Her breathing came hard and fast. Her mind tingled under the brilliant release.

Buck groaned and his cock swelled larger inside of her.

He bucked against her. His groans increased and suddenly his hot seed filled her insides and streamed down her inner legs.

With the completion of their release and with his semi-flaccid cock still buried inside her ass, Buck gently lowered them to the ground.

Exhaustion from their mating claimed them and their breaths intermingled through the warm evening air. His arms trembled as they slid around her waist spooning her against his front.

"That was fabulous," Buck whispered into her ear.

"It was a perfect punishment," she agreed.

Although her ass was sore, she knew she wanted to try this again. And soon.

But not tonight. Tonight she wanted to be with him. To smell his strong masculine scent and feel his powerful body heat snuggle into her every pore.

In the cheerful rays of the late afternoon sun they lay there on the warm ground for a long time, neither of them saying anything.

Eventually they fell asleep.

It was Virgin who heard Joe calling them from somewhere far away. Her eyes popped open and she realized it had gotten late in the day. Wiggling free from Buck's warmth she warned him of their unexpected visitor.

He cursed quietly as they quickly dressed.

A moment later Joe darted into the clearing.

His face was grim enough to set off Virgin's internal alarm.

"What's wrong?" Buck asked as he too sensed something major had happened.

"Ben came back from exploring. He saw something that he wants the two of us to see right now."

"Like what?"

"He didn't say. But whatever it is it has him shaken right down to the bones. Hurry, we have to get back to camp."

* * * * *

"Where do you think they went?" Virgin asked as she paced around the small campfire, rubbing her cold arms frantically trying to break the chill that had claimed her ever since the three brothers had left camp.

"You've asked that question twenty times in the past hour," Jacey mumbled from her perch on a nearby fallen log.

She looked worried. Just like Virgin felt.

"But it's going to be dark soon. They might get lost."

"You heard Ben. He said not to expect them back until late. Maybe even in the morning," she whispered as she continued to stare into the fire.

Another night without Buck lying beside her? It was almost too much to bear.

"Did they hint at where they were going?" Virgin asked again.

She didn't like the uneasiness that had plagued her ever since seeing the worried expression on Joe's face when he'd come to fetch Buck. She needed to know why the three brothers had left so quickly without even a backward glance.

"You were with Ben. What happened? Where did you go?" she prodded.

"I took him to the edge of Freedom Sea to show him the Goddess of Freedom. He took one look at her and I thought he was going to pass out. He said he needed to get his brothers right away."

"Didn't you ask him why he was upset?" Virgin prodded.

"Of course I did. But he's a Hero. Stubborn and secretive."

"And the best lovers," Annie laughed as she emerged from a makeshift shelter of branches the brothers had made to keep the baby's delicate skin protected from the elements.

"Guess who's awake and looking for his mamma."

Virgin's uneasiness slipped the instant Annie handed her the soft baby bundle.

Her son peered up at her with his fantastic blue eyes and his rosebud lips pursed into a smile.

"He drank all his milk?" Virgin asked.

"Every last drop. There's enough left for only one more day. But don't worry. Joe says we'll reach the spaceship tomorrow mid-morning. And they have plenty of milk on board."

The spaceship.

She still couldn't believe that Buck and his brothers were from another planet. When Jacey had told her all about it while Buck had recuperated, Virgin had been shocked to say the least, considering she'd never believed there was life on other planets.

But now that she looked back on it, she should have recognized all the signs that Buck wasn't from The Outer Limits.

He knew how to speak. He was educated but didn't have a clue about her world or about The Outer Limits. But she'd been so preoccupied with curing him of the passion poison, she hadn't really had time to think about his strange behavior.

"He's so cute," Jacey admitted as she played with the baby's fingers. "I've never seen a baby up this close before, y'know. On our field trips to the prisons we were never allowed to go into the nursery. Remember, Virgin?"

"I remember. Now I know why after I had one. It seems it is a female instinct to nurture them." A surge of emotion ripped through Virgin at the memory of waking up in her cell one morning to discover her baby gone. He'd been taken in the dead of night while she'd slept.

"They'd drugged my food that day," Virgin found herself saying. "Drugged me so they could take him without a fight. They must have known I'd fight to keep him. I know it happened to some of the other prisoners."

Annie nodded. "While I was learning to become a doctor, I had to treat several women who'd been released from prison after completing their sentence of giving birth. Most had been severely depressed at having their babies taken from them. One woman in particular had a three-baby sentence. I treated her once when she tried to kill herself after they'd released her from prison. I heard that she eventually succeeded."

Dead silence hung through the camp for a few minutes as Annie's news sunk into the women.

Virgin grew cold at the thought that she'd almost been separated permanently from her son, Kiki. Perhaps she might have killed herself too, if she'd been unable to get him back into her arms.

"The laws of our land need to be changed," Virgin replied firmly.

"How? We're all fugitives now," Jacey said as she tickled the baby's wiggling feet. "Besides, Ben asked me to go with him back to his planet. He says he has a place for us to live."

"Joe wants me to go back with him too," Annie said with sheer excitement.

"We don't need their stupid laws," Jacey chattered gaily.

Virgin swallowed at the sudden lump of dread lodged in her throat. Buck wanted her to go with him too. But could she leave Jarod behind without knowing his fate?

A cold feeling wrapped itself around her shoulders as she peered into the twilight.

Jarod was out there somewhere. She wondered how he was faring. He'd never been away from the hub before. He probably didn't even know where The Outer Limits was.

What if he was recaptured by Cath?

What would his fate be?

Chapter Fifteen

"Kind of seems like the ending of a classic movie I once watched when I was a kid," Buck whispered as he stared at the very tall statue hugging the jagged coastline.

"This is reality, not a damned movie, Buck," Ben snapped.

He didn't blame his brother for being uneasy. It wasn't every day you landed on a faraway planet only to discover a towering statue of a woman wearing a crown, draped in a robe, and holding a torch in one hand and a tablet in the other.

"Sure does look like the Statue of Liberty." He tried to ignore the goosebumps sprouting all over his body as the three of them stood at the base of the statue.

"Nice comparison, Buck," Ben growled.

"Easy, bro. You wouldn't have dragged us down here if you didn't think the same thing yourself," Joe commented as he peered into the open doorway of the moss-covered base.

"Anyone have a flashlight handy? Or a torch?" Buck asked as he joined his brother at the door.

Damp cool air greeted him and all he could see was darkness inside.

"No one is going inside until I take a look," Joe said. He struck a match and stepped inside.

"You think we're in some alternate world to Earth?" Buck wondered aloud, keeping a close eye on Joe. He'd just found his brothers again and he wasn't about to let them disappear into thin air.

"How the hell is it possible that an alternate Earth exists? This *is* the Statue of Liberty. Just look at it. There's no way she can be duplicated. Seven damn rays on her crown. Count them. Seven. Seven continents. The seven seas of the globe. Want to make a bet that flame up there is covered in gold? Huh?"

"No use in getting angry, Ben," Joe's voice echoed from inside the base.

"Why not? We're screwed."

"How so?" Buck asked.

"It's quite simple. " Ben's face was now grim, as if he'd finally come to some sort of unhappy conclusion about their state. "When our spaceship shot through that last wormhole, an unexplored wormhole I might add, we must have gone through a time warp." Ben looked up at the towering statue. "Time could have erased everything familiar to us."

"What do you think happened?" Buck asked, suddenly very uncomfortable with Ben's theory.

"Something major that's for sure. Something that's made the United States into a lush jungle with hot summer weather all the time."

"Maybe Earth got knocked off its axis by some asteroid hitting it?" Buck mused. "Could explain why the geographics for this planet are so similar to Earth when the NASA probe transmitted back those readings before they lost contact with it. Or maybe some massive earthquake or some sort of electrical storm? Earth's always moving through space y'know. Something like this was bound to happen."

"Whatever happened to Earth, it must have been big. Really big," Joe said as he popped back out of the Statue's base. "And if this is the Lady she hasn't done well from the looks of deterioration inside. If Ben's theory is correct and we are in the future then we're very far in the future. And that means only one thing. Everything and everyone we once knew has been erased. Gone. On top of that, we might not be able to get back home."

Alarm sliced through Buck at Joe's forlorn words.

"Why not?" Ben asked tightly.

"Because, if we take our ladies onto the ship and go back to our time, they might be wiped out. They didn't exist back then, remember?"

The chilly goosebumps scrambling through Buck's body made him cold in the late afternoon sunshine.

"But if we came through a time warp into the future, shouldn't we be dead?" Buck pointed out quickly.

"True, but we were in the sleep pods. It probably protected us. And we've only got three pods and no means to make new ones. I won't chance Annie going on the ship now. I won't risk her or our unborn child. I'll stay here. If one or both of you guys wants to go back, I can take care of the women. But remember if you do get back through the wormhole, there's no telling if you'll come out on the other end in the same time frame."

Buck closed his eyes and cursed silently.

"And if you do come out at the other end of the wormhole in the same time frame and you can bring back more pods for the women and myself, it'll be two years at the very least. And we still won't know if it's safe for the women and children. They might disintegrate in the pods.

It's chancy at best but I'll leave it up to each of you. Ben? What do you think?"

"I'm sure as hell not leaving without Jacey and my kid-to-be," Ben said quickly. "And damned if I'm leaving her here on this godforsaken planet without me as protection. No offense. But two men are better than one."

"Buck?" Joe asked.

"Three men are better than one. I'm not going anywhere without Virgin and the little rug rat," Buck replied. "And I won't risk taking them with me. Not unless we know for sure it's safe."

Joe wrapped his arms around both his brothers' shoulders. "Well, younger brothers, it does look like we have a problem."

* * * * *

"What is wrong with you three males?" Virgin snapped as she gazed at the three brothers who sat on the log, their solemn faces illuminated in the camp's lone torchlight.

She'd finally had enough of their odd silence since they'd returned from inspecting the Goddess of Freedom.

She hated to see the three of them sad. She wanted them to be joyful. Like she was happy to finally have her baby back in her arms and Buck once again fucking her.

When no one answered Virgin's question, Jacey chimed in. "What is wrong? Please tell us. You're scaring us with your silence."

"I'd love to know what has happened too," Annie said as she placed another heaping spoonful of potatoes onto Joe's still-full plate.

"We may as well tell them," Buck grumbled as he picked at his meal.

"Tell us what?" Virgin snapped.

"We can't leave this planet. We can't go home," Buck whispered.

"Why not?" All three women asked at the same time.

"That Goddess of Freedom of yours...she's our Statue of Liberty."

Virgin frowned. "I don't understand."

"Before we tell you, I need to ask you one question that all three of us have apparently forgotten to ask...what with everything else that's been going on."

Buck's quiet words shot a warning deep into her heart.

"What do you want to know?"

"What do you call this planet?"

Virgin exhaled a sharp breath. Is that it? They wanted to know the name of their planet?

"Merik," Annie said.

The three brothers exchanged odd glances and Ben closed his eyes and cursed softly.

"As you already know we come from Earth. From a place called The United States of America," Buck said. "Merik and America could be the one and the same. We're already home," Buck explained.

"What do you mean you're already home?" Virgin prodded trying to stifle the uneasiness claiming her senses.

"We believe we might have come through a time warp. We think we might already be on Earth...in the future," Buck explained. "That's why we have to stay here. If we take you through the time warp, you may die."

"I'm willing to take that chance, Buck. I'm sure the others are too," Virgin said as desperation swooped over her like a dark cloud. She didn't want Buck leaving her and the baby here. They were fugitives. It was only a matter of time before the hub sent out a search party for them. If they stayed here they would be discovered and recaptured.

"We want to come with you. We want to stay with you," Virgin whispered.

"We aren't willing to take that chance, Virgin," Joe replied solemnly. "We've discussed it already. We're staying here with you."

Virgin shook her head. "That's not possible. We have to leave. If you don't return to your people they will send out a search party. When they enter our airspace they'll be disintegrated and then more of you will come. There will be a bloodbath."

"Then we'll have to send the ship back without us," Ben replied.

All heads turned to Ben.

"What are you saying?" Buck asked.

"I'm saying we send the ship back, alone. Program a message that says the planet is inhabited by deadly toxins or a deadly plague or something. Tell them that by the time they receive the message we'll all be dead."

Buck frowned. "NASA will buy it, but our family won't."

"There's more of you?" Virgin gasped.

Buck chuckled and winked at her. "Back on Earth we're allowed as many kids as we want. Since Mom and Dad love kids, they started off young and have a good-sized brood."

How many children did Buck want, Virgin found herself wondering. What would be his reaction when she told him she was pregnant? Would he like the idea, or would he hate her for becoming pregnant?

"Okay, so besides a message to NASA that we're dead," Joe continued, "we'll send a message to our family too. A message only they can decipher. We'll tell them what happened. Where we are and why we're staying. We can explain the dangers and warn them that they should not tell anyone we're still alive."

"It might work," Buck agreed.

Virgin looked at Joe for his response. He was nodding in agreement.

"What about you ladies? What do you think?" she asked Annie and Jacey.

"We'll agree. But on one condition," Annie said and cast a stern glance at her male, Joe. "That he eats all the food I've put on his plate."

"Ever the doctor," Joe grinned and began shoveling food into his mouth.

* * * * *

"Do you think it'll work?" Virgin asked as Buck and she stood on the beach three evenings later staring into the night sky.

A message had been sent via a messenger to Jacey's secure contact in the High Five to turn off the disintegration machines that would have prevented the spaceship from leaving the planet. The ship had left hours ago. And from all indications it had made it out of orbit without any problems.

After celebrating their apparent success, everyone had turned in for the night.

Everyone except Buck and herself.

They'd come down to the beach to watch the stars twinkle over Freedom Sea and to listen to the lapping waves.

"It'll work. Joe's idea about putting worms and all the food they can eat into the spaceship sleep pods was a good one. Worms can last through pretty much anything. If they get back to NASA and they're still alive and the family understands the message we sent, then in a couple of years someone in the family will program a ship to come and get us. If the ship doesn't make it back home, they'll send someone from NASA to look for us. There's no telling what'll happen then. We'll just have to not worry and hope for the best."

Virgin shivered with dread. The women on Merik would never allow any males to dominate them ever again. Buck was right. For now she shouldn't worry. It was best to stay positive.

"Do you think your family will understand the messages you sent?"

Buck wrapped an arm around her shoulder and pulled her closer to his warm body.

"They'll understand. We've got lots of family who work at NASA. They'll decipher the code we worked out. Why? You worried about something?"

Virgin held her breath at his question. She could barely contain her delight and her anxiety.

Grabbing his hand she pressed his palm against her abdomen.

"I'm not worried. Just happy to join the rest of the women."

"Doing what?" he asked innocently.

Virgin smiled, "Having babies."

Beside her, he stiffened but didn't say anything.

"How many babies were you planning on having when you were back on Earth, Buck?"

"I don't know. Never really thought about it. Why?" he asked with caution.

"Because I'm seven days pregnant."

"Are you serious?"

Virgin nodded. "Annie confirmed my suspicions three days ago."

His hand spread intimately over her abdomen and he grinned. "I'll be damned. Kiki is going to have a little brother or sister."

Virgin inhaled a sharp breath as his hand trailed lower over her mound. A finger slid erotically between her legs and split her wet labia lips. A shower of beautiful sensations ripped through her cunt as he rubbed seductively against her quickly swelling clit.

"I'm going to like it when you're swollen with my child," he whispered into her ear. "It sure as hell won't stop me from fucking you."

"I've been meaning to ask you, do you have any preference if they are boys or girls?"

"I'll take them as they come," he delicately nibbled on her sensitive earlobe.

"What if they are twins?" Virgin asked.

"Twins, triplets, doesn't matter."

Virgin smiled. "What if they are triplets?"

His intimate nibbling stopped and his head snapped up.

Goddess! Lust and love burned bright in those soft eyes.

"There is a history of triplets in my family, on my dad's side," he said thoughtfully. His eyes brightened in the moonlight. "Are you telling me you already know we're having triplets?"

"I can even tell you the sex from the test Annie gave me."

"Don't tell me! I want it to be a surprise." Buck said quickly.

"So, you aren't shocked at this news? About triplets?"

"What is a shock is the way I'm feeling about you, Virgin. Every time I see you I want you near me. Every time I'm away from you I feel as if a part of me is missing. At first I figured it was the passion poison but now I know it's been in my heart from the instant I saw you. We can have as many triplets as you want, just never leave me, honey."

His head lowered and he caught her in a kiss so fierce, she had to grip his shoulders to keep herself from falling to the beach. But she needn't have held onto him because Buck was already lowering her there, onto the warm sand.

He laid her on her back and gazed down at her. She didn't miss his massive rod bunched tight against his shorts all primed and ready to go.

Yet he hesitated.

"What are you waiting for?"

"I just thought of something. What if I hurt the babies?"

"Annie says they aren't even the size of grapes. You can fuck me as much as you want for a long time still without hurting them."

Indecision brewed in those lusty eyes. "You sure?"

"Yes, please make love to me," Virgin gasped.

She couldn't wait any longer. Couldn't wait until he was buried deep inside of her where he belonged.

And a minute later he was.

THE END

Available in eBook format from Ellora's Cave Publishing, Inc.
www.ellorascave.com

HEROES AT HEART
A HERO ESCAPES

Jan Springer

Preview

Frustration screamed through Queen Jacey's naked body, making her yank hard at the velvet bonds securing her up-stretched arms and spread-eagled legs.

Nothing budged.

She might as well relax. No use in wasting her energy. She'd need all of it when the time came to endure whatever form of sexual torture her enemies, The Breeders, had planned for her.

A whisper of uneasiness tingled up her spine at the sound of footsteps.

Two sets of footsteps.

Okay, two against one. She could handle it. She was a Queen after all, trained to resist torture.

Swallowing the lump of fear clogging her throat, she braced herself against her restraints and kept her eyes glued to the door of the tiny stall they'd brought her to.

Suddenly the door swung open and a male was quickly shoved inside.

Not just any male, but a tall, golden-brown-haired male.

And he was totally naked!

Stormy blue eyes ringed with thick black lashes snapped with desire the instant he saw her. His delicious-looking lips curved upward into an appreciative smile making Jacey's breath back up in her lungs. He had an exquisite masculine face with a straight nose, strong jut to his jawline, and a square chin.

He possessed a sensual neck, broad shoulders and a muscular chest with a generous spattering of curly golden-brown hair that arrowed down over his taut belly and…

Every nerve ending in her body sparked to life as her gaze drew straight to the rock-hard looking balls and the massive eight-inch cock stabbing out at her from between his powerful legs.

Goddess of Freedom!

The male looked so tasty she couldn't wait to wrap her mouth around his thick pulsing rod or kiss his tan nipples.

She blinked in shock.

What in the world was she thinking?

She couldn't allow herself to be fucked by a male.

She had to speak with The Breeders about this. Needed to remind them that queens did not mate with males.

It was unheard of. Scandalous. Illegal.

Absolutely delicious.

Her enemies were about to give her something she'd dreamed about for as long as she could remember.

Why deny herself a taste of her deepest fantasies? Her darkest desires?

About the author:

Jan Springer is the pseudonym for an award winning best selling author who writes erotic romance and romantic suspense at a secluded cabin nestled in the Haliburton Highlands, Ontario, Canada.

She has enjoyed careers in hairstyling and accounting, but her first love is always writing. Hobbies include kayaking, gardening, hiking, traveling, reading and writing.

Jan welcomes mail from readers. You can write to her c/o Ellora's Cave Publishing at 1337 Commerce Drive, Suite 13, Stow OH 44224.

Also by Jan Springer:

Heroes at Heart: *A Hero's Welcome*

Heroes at Heart: *A Hero Escapes*

Outlaw Lovers: *Jude Outlaw*

Why an electronic book?

We live in the Information Age—an exciting time in the history of human civilization in which technology rules supreme and continues to progress in leaps and bounds every minute of every hour of every day. For a multitude of reasons, more and more avid literary fans are opting to purchase e-books instead of paperbacks. The question to those not yet initiated to the world of electronic reading is simply: *why?*

1. *Price.* An electronic title at Ellora's Cave Publishing runs anywhere from 40-75% less than the cover price of the exact same title in paperback format. Why? Cold mathematics. It is less expensive to publish an e-book than it is to publish a paperback, so the savings are passed along to the consumer.
2. *Space.* Running out of room to house your paperback books? That is one worry you will never have with electronic novels. For a low one-time cost, you can purchase a handheld computer designed specifically for e-reading purposes. Many e-readers are larger than the average handheld, giving you plenty of screen room. Better yet, hundreds of titles can be stored within your new library—a single microchip. (Please note that Ellora's Cave does not endorse any specific brands. You can check our website at www.ellorascave.com for customer

recommendations we make available to new consumers.)

3. *Mobility.* Because your new library now consists of only a microchip, your entire cache of books can be taken with you wherever you go.
4. *Personal preferences are accounted for.* Are the words you are currently reading too small? Too large? Too...**ANNOYING**? Paperback books cannot be modified according to personal preferences, but e-books can.
5. *Innovation.* The way you read a book is not the only advancement the Information Age has gifted the literary community with. There is also the factor of what you can read. Ellora's Cave Publishing will be introducing a new line of interactive titles that are available in e-book format only.
6. *Instant gratification.* Is it the middle of the night and all the bookstores are closed? Are you tired of waiting days—sometimes weeks—for online and offline bookstores to ship the novels you bought? Ellora's Cave Publishing sells instantaneous downloads 24 hours a day, 7 days a week, 365 days a year. Our e-book delivery system is 100% automated, meaning your order is filled as soon as you pay for it.

Those are a few of the top reasons why electronic novels are displacing paperbacks for many an avid reader. As always, Ellora's Cave Publishing welcomes your questions and comments. We invite you to email us at service@ellorascave.com or write to us directly at: 1337 Commerce Drive, Suite 13, Stow OH 44224.

Printed in the United States
25544LVS00003B/70-489